I0524007

Pierz Newton-John lives in Melbourne. In addition to being a writer, he is a guitarist, web developer, former psychotherapist and father. His stories have appeared extensively in Australian literary journals and anthologies including *Meanjin*, *Overland*, *New Australian Stories*, *Kill Your Darlings* and *The Sleepers Almanac*. He won the Alan Marshall Award in 2008 for 'This Old Man'. His first novel is in progress.

Pierz Newton-John

Fault Lines

spineless wonders

www.shortaustralianstories.com.au

Spineless Wonders
BN01164417
PO Box 220
STRAWBERRY HILLS
New South Wales, Australia, 2012
www.shortaustralianstories.com.au

First published by Spineless Wonders 2012

Edited by Linda Godfrey. Copyediting & layout by Bronwyn Mehan.

Typeset in Adobe Garamond Pro

Printed and bound by Lightning Source Australia

National Library of Australia Cataloguing-in-Publication entry

Fault Lines/Pierz Newton-John; illustrations by Paden Hunter
1st ed.
9780987089762 (pbk.)
Hunter, Paden
A823.4

For Os

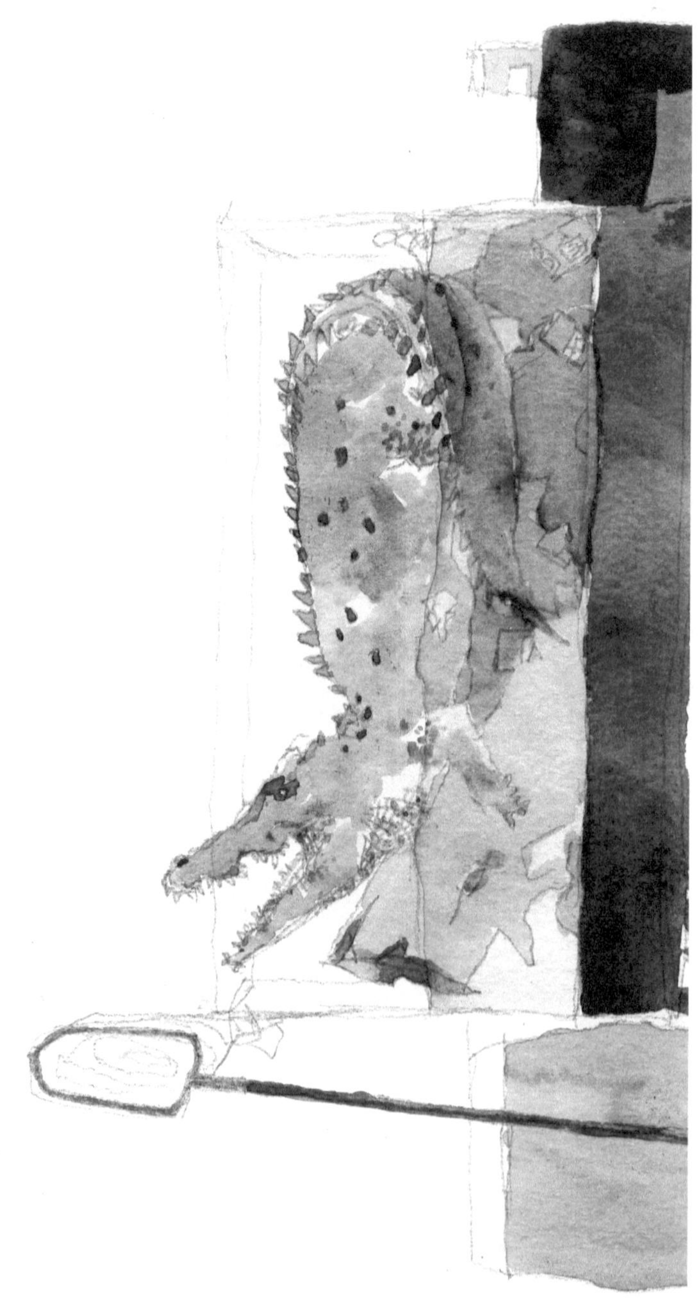

Contents

Eliot's Awakening

In the carpark behind Jim's PC World, Eliot was having a smoko with a couple of the part-time gophers. In an attempt to impress J. Edgar, they were seeing who could punch a hole in the side of one of the cardboard boxes that were stacked up outside the loading bay. J. Edgar was a pretty Greek girl, with a single flaw: she had the hugest nostrils Eliot had ever laid eyes on. He was unaware of her real name. She had been J. Edgar ever since he'd worked there. If she hated being called this, she never complained, although she did cover herself in a cloak of icy disdain that may or may not have had something to do with the insulting nickname. While the boys puffed out their skinny chests and took turns stepping up to the battered boxes, she leaned against a car ten metres away, staring into space and blowing smoke up, up and away.

When Eliot stepped towards the boxes and made a fist, Donald—a short, fat sixteen-year-old kid with the kind of fine red hair he was sure to lose by twenty-five—laughed out loud. 'Ooh,' he stirred, 'that's really threatening.' Eliot flushed and had a momentary impulse to smack him in the lip. He may not have been the most macho of specimens, but there was still something intolerably galling about having his fists mocked by a nerdy gopher two years his junior. In fact, Eliot had been taking Wing Chun classes for a year and he rather fancied himself against the boxes, but when he punched, it was a pathetic, unco flail that only made Donald laugh harder. Embarrassed, he shot a glance at J. Edgar, but she was a million miles away, chewing down her pink lacquered fingernails and staring into the shimmery haze that the heat made over the road.

'Hey. We got customers. Butt your ciggies and get your arses in here.' Nathan, the sales manager, was leaning out of the doorway. Everyone hopped to it and in a moment the carpark was empty except for Eliot, who dawdled over the last centimetre of tobacco in his cigarette before finally grinding the butt out on the roof of one of the company cars. It was bloody hot, had been all January. Sweat trickled inside his cheap grey suit. He leaned back on the car to breathe in the moment of solitude before he went back in to face the customers and their incessant demands.

At Jim's PC World, salesmen were like sharks. They had to remain in perpetual forward motion. Jim had an uncanny radar for stationary employees. As soon as one came to a standstill, he'd appear, demanding to know what they were doing to justify their continued employment. There were times when there was not much to do, and at these moments, the only way Eliot had found to avoid his attentions was to adopt a purposeful, charging gait and do circuits of the showroom, workshop and storeroom. After a while, he settled into a pleasant rhythm and could dream off. In fact, he did a few laps whenever he got tired of serving customers.

He'd watch the clock, baffled by its Einsteinian capacity to slow to a near-stop between the hours of three and five. But then, when the moment of freedom arrived, he'd stand at the bus-stop wondering what the hell he'd been looking forward to. Eliot's home life was sad. Sad in the loser sense. His dad had split for Queensland with, can you believe it, his secretary, and his mum had quickly repartnered with a poker machine. 'What are you looking at?' she'd bark from the mirror, lipstick hovering momentarily away from her mouth. 'Why do you bother? It's not like you're gonna talk to anyone,' Eliot would answer. She'd snort, make a cat's bum of her mouth again and finish the lippy. Then with a final tease of her hair she'd be out the door: 'Dinner's in the freezer.' He'd open the fridge to find a pack of Birds Eye fish fingers and frozen peas. *Oh yeah, thanks for that, Mum.* So he'd order in a pizza. Not that it was much better—all those half-cold worms of ham.

The absence of his parents left him at the mercy of his older brother Troy, whom nobody except Eliot seemed to have noticed was turning into a mental case. For weeks the smell of piss in the house had grown—so gradually that, like frogs in a slowly heated beaker, they had adjusted to it without comment. Then came the inevitable moment at which the point of supersaturation was reached, and all the stench precipitated at once into their mother's consciousness. Suddenly she was screaming, 'Why must I live in a men's urinal?' and running around sniffing everything like a bloodhound gone berserk. It turned out Troy had been pissing in the pot plant outside his room because he couldn't be bothered making the trip to the toilet at the other end of the house. The plant—a sensitive, ferny creature—was fading fast. Its feathery hands were upturned in surrender as it prepared to depart this world.

'Are you responsible for this?' she yelled when she discovered the source of the stink. Troy just leaned insolently in his doorway, a pout of childish defiance on his face. When she ditched the dying fern into the bin, he kicked his bedroom door so hard he broke the hinge. 'I *needed* that plant!' he shouted.

His mother went gambling, and Troy stuck his head into a plastic bag full of Araldite. Eliot found him in the garage, flaked out on Mitzy's sofa, so-called because it had once belonged to their dog, before she was run over. The vapours were dizzying. 'Bitch,' he slurred, looking straight through Eliot with irises the blue of half-dried glue. 'Dad was right to leave. Stupid fucking bitch and her fucking pokies.'

A few days later, Eliot had caught him trying to give himself a blow job (never was the term more inapt) with their mother's new high-powered vacuum cleaner. As soon as Troy kicked the power on, the thing nearly tore his balls off and he let out a howl alarming enough to drag Eliot away from *Age of Empires*, even though it meant losing the game and a consequent drop in his online rating. Apparently the pain had overwhelmed Troy's problem-solving abilities, because he was still screaming over the unnaturally high whine of the machine when Eliot burst in and pulled the power cord from the socket. He knew better than to laugh at his brother rolling on the floor crying and clutching his frankfurter-pink cock, swearing Eliot to eternal silence.

Eliot was often kept awake by the sound of gunfire and the screams of dying men. He'd swear and roll over, pressing his pillow around his head to cover his ears. Silence would fall for a while and a sweet dreaminess would creep over him. He'd be sliding deliciously into the pool of sleep when a machine gun would start up, and a cut-off shriek would wrench him back to wakefulness. 'Fuck!' he'd shout at the wall. 'It's two o'clock!' The wall would remain silent, apart from a few muffled pistol shots. Occasionally there'd be a crash and a burst of swearing as Troy threw his joystick against something. This would go on until sheer exhaustion dragged Eliot under.

He was packing shelves in the storeroom, noting with curiosity the new fish-tank Jim had installed. Some of the fish were so garish and unusual that it left Eliot feeling quite puzzled. One of them walked on the bottom of the tank like a neon-legged spider. His confusion had a familiarity about it, but he could not quite pin it down.

'Hi, Eliot. Need a hand?' J. Edgar had appeared in the doorway.

'Sure,' Eliot replied, a little surprised. Normally she was so stand-offish.

She came forward and started putting software onto the shelves, leaning over Eliot as she did, so close that her breasts almost brushed his face.

'J. Edgar,' he said, lightly.

'Yes, honey.'

'Why are you in your underwear?' His suspicions were growing.

'Hmmm?' she murmured, her lips brushing his ear, one hand planting itself on his thigh. It was unbearably sweet.

He remembered the weird fish and a light went on, a deeply disappointing one. 'Hang on! I know what's going on. This is a dream, isn't it?'

She looked disbelieving, offended. 'No, honey, I swear.' The bra evaporated.

Ah, what the hell, he'd never have another chance; he grabbed her and started kissing her. It was bliss, but then he noticed something was wrong; her breast felt flat and too hard, her arm too strong. He pulled away and with a surge of horror realised it was Nathan the sales manager he was kissing. But it was too late to stop the uncontrollable spurting in his loins that woke him, sticky and sweating in his bed.

'Oh, God!' he moaned. 'Now I'm turning gay!'

It was the confirmation he had been dreading ever since their most recent sales meeting. Jim's automated sales-tracking and charting software showed the trajectory of each of the staff's accumulating sales through the month. The chart was divided into colour-coded 'performance zones'. Nathan's line soared rocket-like far into the blue empyrean at the top of the chart. Way down below it, the other salesmen tracked like droning Cessnas through a band of mediocre grey. Eliot breathed a sigh of relief. He had expected worse.

'Congratulations, Nathan,' Jim beamed as the graph appeared. 'Once again, your performance is stratospheric.' Then he turned to Eliot. 'Eliot. Your performance is … to be truthful, it's egregious.'

'Thank you.'

'It's terrible.'

'Oh.'

Jim fingered the screen, pointing out a line so close to the x-axis that Eliot had failed to notice it before. It beetled almost horizontally across the band of red at the bottom of the screen.

Jim shook his head sadly. 'Let's say a customer comes into the shop and tells you he's looking for a computer for his kids. What's the first thing you say?'

Eliot floundered. He looked at Nathan, who tried to mouth something without moving his lips. It was like trying to lip-read a ventriloquist. 'You're a very generous man?' he ventured at last.

'NO! *When are you looking to buy!* How many times do I have to tell you this stuff, Eliot? There are three key questions: How can I help you? When are you looking to buy? How much do you want to spend? Is that really so hard to remember?'

Nathan coughed. 'Err, Jim, if I could just say something here?'

'Certainly, Nathan.'

'I think there may be another explanation for Eliot's figures. As far as I can tell, he's actually pretty good with the three key questions.' Eliot gave him a startled look. This was news to him. 'But he's not selfish enough. He's almost made some great sales this month, but then he's left me to close the sale. So to be honest, I don't think the graph represents the true picture.'

That was when Eliot first felt it—the algedonic twang in his chest like someone had just cut a very small piano wire, a feeling of pathetic, embarrassing adoration. And—was it true? Did he really feel it?—prickling in his groin. It was so dreadful. On top of everything else he was turning into a poof.

He'd always thought something like this was going to happen to him. It was just his luck. Ever since Miles Valiant had been struck down suddenly by homosexuality after he left school, Eliot had worried that it might get him too. For ages everyone envied Miles because he was going out with Samantha Willis, the school's second hottest girl. Then, the year after school finished, he'd broken it off with Samantha, drifted out of contact with everyone, and then Geoff McKinley had seen him outside the Peel, in a white tank-top.

After the sales meeting, Nathan drove Eliot home in his hotted-up, turbo-charged Commodore SS. When they turned off Studley Park Road onto the Boulevard he put his foot to the floor, and the car shot forward with a vicious growl, leaving Eliot's stomach lurching to catch up.

As they went round the first bend at close to 100 ks, the tyres skittered over the road surface, the rear of the car slewing a little before pulling itself back into line. Eliot clutched the dash, his feet making futile braking motions. He tried closing his eyes, but it only made things worse. He looked at Nathan and saw that he was extracting a cigarette from his pocket with one hand while he took the turns with the other. Once it was in his mouth he started to fumble with the cigarette lighter in the dash. Eliot lost it. 'I'll do it!' he shrieked. 'Just fucking drive!' He batted Nathan's hand away and pulled out the lighter, held it up to the fag hanging from Nathan's mouth.

'Thanks, mate,' said Nathan round the side of the cigarette, Humphrey Bogart-style.

'Can I have one too?' Eliot asked.

'Sure.' Nathan chucked the Peter Jacksons into his lap and Eliot plucked one out and lit up, sucking in the smoke like an asthmatic with an inhaler. The nicotine rush instantly soothed his mind, and suddenly he felt sanguine about the prospect of death.

'Hey, thanks for today,' he said. 'You didn't need to lie to cover for me.'

'Nah, that's alright. But I can't keep Jim off your back forever you know.'

'Yeah, I know. I'm getting better ... I think.'

'Hey, look!' Nathan pointed at two super-fit, gym-inflated figures emerging from the trees near the side of the road.

'What?'

'You know what this is along here?'

'What? A jogging track? No, what do you mean?'

'It's a beat.'

'A beat?'

'A gay beat.'

'You mean they ...'

'Yep.'

Eliot was silent, taking it in, looking at the trees in a whole new sinister light. The previously scenic stretch of road now seemed full of cloying, phobic horror. It pullulated invisibly with obscene, muscular acts, moustaches, gargantuan penises. He felt a wave of carsickness.

When they pulled up outside his place, Nathan turned to him. 'Say, what you doing Saturday night? You wanna go clubbing with me and some of me mates?'

He felt it again, that pang in his chest, that little chiming note of pathos and something that might have been love. He hated clubbing, but he felt a pathetic gratitude for the invitation.

'Sure. That'd be cool.'

When he got inside, his mother was sitting at the kitchen table. The table was strewn with bills, most of them in colour. Her face was a wreck of dribbling mascara and haggard lines.

'Hi, Ellie!' she said with a ghastly smile.

He started to tell her not to call him that, then his shoulders slumped in defeat. 'How much do you need?' he said in a dead voice.

'Only a few hundred, sweetie, just to cover the mortgage. You know, it's all your dad's fault. He hasn't paid me a cent of maintenance since he left. If I ever see that bastard again I'll kill him, I swear it.'

'Mum, I'm an adult now. He doesn't have to pay maintenance.'

'I had a bad night Ell, that's all. Someone was sitting at my lucky machine. I knew it was a bad idea to play on a different one. So stupid! I broke all my rules. I smoked with my left hand. I didn't even wipe the chair before I sat down ...'

'Listen to yourself!'

'Please, Eliot!' She took hold of his sleeve, her eyes looking up at him in such a desperate, beggarly fashion that he felt a surge of confused emotions: disgust, love, hate, pity, fear. He shook off her hand and threw his pay packet onto the kitchen table. As he slammed the door behind him, he heard her voice calling after him, 'I'll pay you back. Next pay. I promise, okay?'

In the darkened corridor outside his room, Troy was lurking, silhouetted against the blue computer-screen light from his room.

'Payday today, right?'

'I don't have anything. I gave it all to Mum.'

'Bullshit!' The hulking figure came towards him fast. Eliot tried to dodge past him to his room, but Troy caught his arm in a bruising grip. 'Give it,' he snarled. He seemed to be growing more thuggish and stupid by the day. Eliot could smell solvent fumes and body odour.

'I told you …' He tried to shake off his brother's hand, but it was too strong. Troy had inherited genes for muscle bulk that had completely bypassed Eliot. His other hand now began to force its way into the pockets of Eliot's trousers. Eliot fought and kicked, but it only made Troy more violent; he rammed Eliot against the wall with his weight, pinning him there while his hands groped in his pockets for the cash. Eliot began to sob, but it was only when Troy had gone through every pocket that his body went slack and released him.

'You little shit,' he whined. 'Why'd you give her the money? Don't you know she'll only blow it on the pokies?'

Eliot swallowed back salt. 'Yeah, and I suppose you were going to invest it in your super …' he spat. He retreated into his room and slammed the door.

Eliot had once heard that every moment of our lives is perfectly recorded in our memory, and that it is only our capacity to access those records at will that is limited. If this was true, he figured he had within his internal archives kilometres of the world's dullest archival footage of his father. Dad reading the newspaper. Dad yawning. Dad picking his nose. Dad going down the corridor. Dad mowing the lawn. Dad saying, 'Cathy, what the, uh, what did the weather say? Bugger, looks like I won't be able to work on the shed today ...' Loads of boring, incoherent rubbish like that. Miles of it, spools and spools all over the cutting-room floor of his unconscious. This, he figured, was the true history of his relationship with his father. And yet, out of all these endless, unwatchable reels, there were just a few seconds that for whatever reason got replayed over and over, until the film itself was worn out, faded with over exposure. Perhaps even falsified by subtle distortions and alterations that he unconsciously introduced with each viewing.

One such film clip: His dad took him down to the Mornington Peninsula to fish. For some reason that Eliot could no longer recall, Troy was not there. Was he sick? They went out on a pier in the early morning and sat in silence, their lines dangling into a sluggish sea that gently slapped the rotted pillars. They never usually caught anything, and Eliot would feel as bored as the seagulls that stood around in listless hope of a scrap. But today, he felt a mysterious potency in him, that golden presence so worshipped by the Chinese and which we prosaically call 'luck'. He caught a fish, a magnificent, improbable fish, a pinkie snapper that weighed nearly four kilograms. It came out of the water thrashing, resisting him like all miracles do, a shimmering lode of luck almost too heavy for his arms to reel in. But the moment that he replayed through the projector of his mind over and over, the moment faded almost to transparency, but still able to leave a certain singing resonance in his heart, was the look on his father's face when he brought that mighty fish up onto the pier between them.

It was odd, but after that day he could not recall going fishing with him ever again.

Sitting in a corner of the upper lounge at the Metro, sipping a rum and coke, he remembered why he hated clubbing. The massive amplifiers blasted out a noise so loud it obliterated thought. The beat pounded his head with giant, weightless blows, while a disco ball on the ceiling speared his eye with migrating shards of light. He breathed sweat, alcohol, aftershave, perfume. The dance floor below heaved and thumped under rivers of ultraviolet. Nathan and two of his mates, Dave and Andrew, sat opposite him, beers in hand. Nathan leaned towards him.

'Eee ooo aaa aa oh oh ooh ay?'

'What?!' he shouted back.

'Eee ooo aaa aa oh oh ooh ay?'

'Can't HEAR you!'

'Eee ooo aaa dance floor ooh ooh okay?'

'No worries!' He'd already spent half an hour thrashing about to the music like an electrocuted monkey, getting elbowed in the head by an over-sized Greek in the throes of Dionysian abandonment and wondering whether anyone was watching him and how stupid he looked. 'I'll be right here!'

Nathan and the others got up and squeezed into the crowd, leaving Eliot in the solitary embrace of his lounge chair. Two girls fell into the empty places they left. One was pretty, the other beautiful in a toxic, Los Angeles kind of way. With her perfect little retroussé nose, her plumped-up, golden breasts, her sharky little mouth with its even rows of teeth, she was gorgeous and awful. She flicked her lissotrichous locks over her shoulder every seven seconds. She rolled her eyes in shock-horror: no waaay! He watched her laugh through the wall of sound that separated her from him as if through glass. The mixed drinks tasted of nothing. He was drinking pure space. His face was numb.

When they spilled down Bourke Street at two a.m., his ears were ringing and deadened, his vision dimmed with alcohol. He heard himself laughing.

'Ooh that girl, dude!' Nathan was saying. 'She wanted it Eliot, I'm telling you. The way she looked at you! She wanted to sit on your face.' Eliot knew it was bullshit, but the laugh kept hacking out of his throat. 'And she was hot. Like fucking seriously.'

'Yeah, man,' said Dave. 'Pussy was in the bag. You fucken blew it.'

They piled into the Commodore. It smelled of cold and cigarettes.

'You gonna drive me home now?' Eliot asked. It occurred to him that Nathan must be way over the limit, but the thought struck him from a remote distance, as concerning as someone else's burglar alarm.

'Home? Like shit! The night is yet young.' Nathan spun the car out of its parking spot and fishtailed down the street. He looked at his mates. 'We got a tradition anyway for Saturday nights. Can't go home yet. It wouldn't be right.' They started to laugh. Their three faces turned towards him, expressions expectant but unreadable.

'Okay cool, whatever.'

He was too tired, too blind to worry about Nathan's driving. His face fell against the window and the nightlife rolled past like a dream. He was almost dozing when he realised they were on Kew Boulevard, not driving at breakneck speed this time, but cruising, almost at a crawl. He came awake suddenly, anxiety coagulating in his guts. Everyone was quiet now, the only sound the predatory rumble of the engine.

He tried to speak, but when he got the words out, they came out in a squeaky child's voice. 'What are we doing?'

The silence extended so long he thought no-one was going to answer. Then Nathan turned to look at him again. 'How's your Wing Chun going?'

Almost as soon as he said it, Andrew started to shout. 'There! There!' He pointed into the headlights. Someone was emerging from the trees.

A young man's face, bleached of detail by the halogen headlamps, turned towards them, a hand going up to shelter his eyes against the brilliance. He hesitated, and in that moment the car doors burst open and Dave and Andrew jumped out. The man turned and ran. Nathan wrenched up the handbrake and, in the split second before he gave chase too, turned to Eliot. 'Come on! There's only one of them. It'll be easy. We'll hold him and you can kick.'

Eliot sat in the car, the doors open, cold air blowing through, the engine still running. Saliva flooded his mouth and he rolled out into the gutter and vomited. From his knees, crouched over the sour stinking puddle, he looked up. He couldn't see anyone, just the trees in the headlights, twisted and ghostly, their shadows growing gigantic as they spilled down the empty road.

A cheerful jingle—'Copacabana' or something—woke Eliot from a deep sleep. He fumbled his phone out of his pocket to see it was an '07' number, Queensland.

'Eliot?' It took him a moment to recognise the voice as his father's.

Apparently things hadn't worked out with the secretary. Apparently he realised he'd made a terrible mistake. He wanted Eliot to talk to his mother, find out if she'd have him back. Act as a peace-maker, broker the truce, that kind of thing. He was a fool. You don't know what you got till it's gone, that's what Joni Mitchell said, and you know what? He never knew how right she was. Anyway, how was everyone? How was Cathy? How was Troy? How was Mitzy?

'They're all fine, Dad, fine. Everything's fine, and all Mum keeps talking about is how much she wants you back. I think you should surprise her. She'd be thrilled to death.'

'Really?' It was all too good to be true. He'd pack his things right away.

'Fine, Dad, you do that. Maybe we can have a party.'

'You're a good lad, Eliot.' He heard just a moment of hesitation in his father's voice, a crack in his stupidity quickly plastered over by his eagerness to believe. 'I knew I could rely on you.'

'Yeah, likewise.' He hung up.

Outside the bus window, brown fields rolled past, a drab spectacle. Perhaps not the shining omen of a bold new future he might have hoped for. Then he saw a green sign up ahead. *Sydney, 140.* That, at least, gave him cause to smile.

Shock

Smithy meets the girl at the pub one Friday night, when his workmates have all gone home, and he's the only one left at the bar, watching the foam slide down the inside of his glass. She comes to stand beside him and he feels her eyes on him. Her blackness is shocking and out of place in this white man's pub; a different kind of blackness from that of the Aborigines who occasionally slouch along the bar. Skin like polished night, against which the hot pink of her top looks bright as candy, her breasts provocatively emphasised.

When he makes eye contact, she offers him a hesitant but warm smile.

'Danny?' She gives the name an American twang.

Wow, he thinks, a real—what do they call themselves now?—African-American, just like on TV. And so beautiful, so young. But who the hell is Danny? One thing is for sure, it's not him. When was the last time anybody smiled at him like that, so hopefully and openly, as if he contained so many possibilities? He thinks he'd give just about anything to be this Danny character, the one that smile is meant for. Then, almost as soon as that thought occurs to him, it is chased by another, darker idea, and before he has time to think twice, before the faltering smile has a chance to leave her face completely, he turns on his own most charming smile, full of all the sincerity he can muster.

'Hi. Yes, I'm Danny. How are you?'

The doubt evaporates from her face and the wavering smile returns to take full possession of her features. She reveals brilliant white teeth, and inside her cushiony lips, a line of pink like the inside of a conch.

She reaches out her hand with a charming awkwardness. 'Hi! I'm Carla.' Her palm is smooth and dry to the touch, pale as if it had been sanded back.

'Of course,' he says.

'It's so great to meet you!' She settles on the stool beside him and plonks her handbag on the bar. 'I wasn't sure if it was you for a moment—that was such a bad photo you sent.'

'Yeah, sorry about that,' Smithy smiles, and signals the barman. 'Can I get you something?'

'Sure. A G&T?'

The barman mixes the drink, and Smithy pushes a tenner over the counter.

'So. How've you been?'

'Okay—oh you know, bored as ever! You were right—I should never have taken that house so far away from the city. It's such a hole!' She laughs. Despite her friendliness, he detects an edge of nerves in the way she latches onto her drink, her slightly gabbling speech.

She launches into a diatribe against the suburb, the house she lives in, the stares she endures buying groceries at the local supermarket—'So rude, like they never saw a black person before'—and he thanks his lucky stars she gets talkative when anxious rather than clamming up. He's quickly able to fill in that she's a student, studying microbiology or something, here only until the end of the year before she has to go back to the States. She only flew in a month ago. She's staying in a student flop way out in the northern suburbs with a couple of other international students. They live on a main road near an intersection, and each night she hears the diesel trucks lurch away from the lights, shift gears like they're gulping for air, and roar past her window. It took a week before she could get any sleep. Every time she started to drift off, she'd be jolted awake by the vivid hallucination that they were headed right at her, that her bed had somehow been displaced into the middle of the road.

'And you?' she asks him. 'How are you? How are the kids treating you?'

Kids? For a moment his mind spins as he tries to compose a response vague enough to cover all possibilities.

'Oh, the same, you know,' he says, smiling indulgently as if to say *kids will be kids!*

'I don't know how you put up with them. I could never be a teacher.'

He shrugs philosophically. 'It's a job.'

'Come on, you love it.'

He forces a smile that he hopes looks suitably modest. 'I guess ... yeah, you're right. I do. '

A little while later she goes to the toilet and leaves her handbag on the bar. As soon as she's out of sight he opens it and fishes around among her belongings until he finds her mobile. He quickly flicks through her most recent texts until he finds one with the name 'Danny'.

Hey Carla. Looking 4wd 2 it. Will b gr8 2 meet u at last.

He thumbs 'reply' and taps in a short message, his heart pounding:

Sorry, not coming 2nite. Really sorry, i met someone. Pls dont contact me again. C.

He hits 'send', then goes to her sent items and deletes the record of the message. It all takes less than a minute, and he's sipping his beer casually when she returns, the phone safely tucked away again. Now he just has to hope this Danny character is man enough to take it and not send some abusive or pleading reply.

'Well?' she says when she gets back. 'Shall we get some dinner then?'

Smithy's grin broadens. 'I thought you'd never ask. I'm hungry as a wolf.'

And Smithy is hungry. Smithy is ravenous. Because two years ago—can it really be two years?—his wife left him, and he hasn't had a woman since. Not a kiss even, barely a glance, when once they couldn't get enough of him. What? Does his loneliness stink? He gave Melissa ten years, the better part of his youth, and then she left him while he was away on a day-trip to the Gold Coast for business. He came back and the house was a shell, doors banging open, that was how fast she'd run, and even the furniture gone. Nothing, just his clothes on the rack, the CDs of his she'd hated. Kids' rooms empty. In the kitchen on the floor he found a butter knife with a bent-tipped blade that she must have dropped when she was packing, in the bedroom a bra, and in one room the wooden bee on a string that his boy used to drag about when he was two. With the wings that spun and went clacketty clack.

Those three things she left haunted him. In the end he was convinced there was no mistake after all. She planned each one as carefully as the escape itself. Either she plotted it or God did, not that he believed in God. The bee, that was for the kids of course. The cruellest sting. And what could you do about it? Throw it out? How could you? Smash it? No, you sat on the floor and you drank and you pulled the string, over and over, and the wings turned and went clacketty clack. Then the bra. Well figure that one out, Einstein. No prizes. It smelt clean, like a bed freshly made before you roll in it. No trace of her scent on it, just the empty cups, the what-do-you-call, negative space.

And then the knife. That was a good one. That was the punch line. Stick it in and twist. He'd hold it in the venetian striped streetlight shine in the long pissed hours, turning the blade to catch the flash of neon strip and laugh. Thumb the blunt serration where the tip bent from someone's long-ago effort to prise open a jar of pickles and think, I gotta hand it to you. Goddamn butter knife. She might have left something sharper.

Two years later he was working again, back in a retail salesroom selling cameras. He'd moved out of the old house into a one-bedroom shoebox, gone back to the gym, even signed up on an internet dating site. But the only women who showed any interest in him were old and used up, and had their own stink of desperation. The worst time was three a.m. That was when he'd have the dream, of rooms beyond rooms beyond rooms, and every one of them empty. He'd wake and in that low-tide of the soul the reefs of his pain—rage and hunger and despair—would stand out bare and jagged and completely unchanged from the last time. The immutable bedrock of his life.

Now they're sitting on cushions in the plush warmth of a Thai restaurant and Carla has ordered herself Pad Phuk or something, and when he's talking about how much he loves helping the kids at school, helping them get a better start in life, she reaches out and touches his hand. It looks so white next to hers, garish and old, the hand of a corpse, and he wonders how she can bear to touch it.

'You're a good man, Danny,' she says. 'That is a rare thing.'

'No, I'm not,' he says, but she shakes her head.

'No, you are,' she insists. 'I could tell that from your emails, the kindness in them. You're gentle and you're wise. You're different.'

And what can Smithy say to that?

He finds himself putting up his hand to order a bottle of wine, against his better judgement, which tells him he'll need his wits about him if he's going to pull this off. He thinks maybe he catches a surprised look from Carla, though she doesn't say anything. Who knows, maybe in his emails he said he was a teetotaller. He notices a dangerous stab of recklessness, an urge to shock her with some outrageously cynical remark. That acid tongue, that edge of danger was always part of his attractiveness to women when he was younger. Danny—this cheesy-postcard, kiddie-loving SNAG who probably believes in yoga and fairies and the manifesting power of crystals—is such a badly fitting garb. The sudden image of the wolf in 'Little Red Riding Hood' makes him grin. What big teeth you have, Danny. He can feel his old savage loquacity gurgling in the rusted pipe of his throat, and all he needs to do is turn the tap. Then he looks at the smooth dark swell of Carla's cleavage. Easy does it, big guy. He fills her wine glass close to the brim and smiles.

She lifts the glass, holds it out in the air in front of her and he brings his own to meet it, a slightly too solid clink that threatens to upset the finely balanced liquid.

'To ... what?' he says, allowing just a hint of suggestiveness to slide into the gaze which meets hers.

'To new friends?'

The word 'friends' doesn't please him, but he nods and takes a gulp. 'Sure. To new friends.'

Carla sips, regarding him over the edge of her glass.

'You're different to how I thought.'

Smithy keeps his voice light. 'How so?'

'Just different. Older for starters. How old are you?'

He spontaneously rounds down by a few years. 'Thirty-five. Does it bother you?'

'No. I don't believe in age. Everything you said in your emails I could so totally relate to, you know? I made a decision before I even met you that you were ...' she stops, embarrassed.

'What?'

Her eyes drop bashfully. 'I don't know. Right. For me.'

Smithy fancies he can see the blush, even through her black skin. He leans forward over his hardening cock. 'That's so weird,' he says. 'So did I.'

'Really?' She looks up, her eyes shining, her wine-wet lips stretching away from the neat, pretty rows of her teeth.

'Absolutely. I knew ...'

He watches her struggle to moderate her smile, to reshape its childish excitement into something composed and womanly. How old is she, anyway? Surely no older than twenty-two, twenty-three. Yet there is an even younger quality about her, something unformed and naive, and Smithy feels an unwelcome flicker of letdown, as if maybe this is all too easy.

Later, he is driving her along the freeway, out into unfamiliar suburbs, the pedestrian bridges above the road adorned with advertisements for airlines and credit cards. It's late and the suburbs look abandoned apart from the trucks, the all-night servos, a McDonald's, empty too but illuminated like a surreal doll's house in a parody of the welcome of home. A cloned piece of America planted out here next to the highway.

There's somewhere she wants to show him, she says. To his annoyance, she won't tell him what it is—a surprise, she reckons. They drive further, into the ugly desolation beyond the suburbs.

'Here—see that little turn-off just ahead?'

It's just a break in the fence that borders the road, only some muddy tyre tracks spreading onto the tarmac indicating there is a turn-off there at all. The headlights spill onto gravel, mud, tufts of stubble. He pulls up, and the lights beam sightlessly into nothingness: a chain-link fence then an abyss of darkness.

'What's this?'

She gets out of the car. 'You'll see. Come on.'

Smithy cuts the engine and gets out after her. It's so cold, he can see his breath. Stars too, despite the dirty smear of light from the city, the rim of flickering suburbs. Surely she didn't bring him here for this pitiful handful of stars?

'Carla?'

'Just be patient.'

'It's cold. There's nothing here.'

'Just wait, Danny.'

He stifles a pulse of impatience that surges through his limbs, keeps the smile edgily on his face.

'Okay. You're the boss.'

He moves towards her darkened silhouette, wraps his arms around her from behind. Her frizzy curls prickle against his chin like steel wool.

Ahead in the sky, a point of light low on the horizon that he'd taken for Venus is brightening, growing. It's an aeroplane—he can now see the lights flashing along its wings. At first he watches it idly, then it dawns on him that it's headed right at them, moving neither up nor down in his field of vision, but growing larger and brighter by the second. It looms exponentially, becomes a jumbo jet, coming in so close and low that for an irrational moment he thinks it's going to crash right into them. He yelps and lets go of Carla, putting up his hands in a helpless gesture of self-protection as it bears down like a gigantic bird of prey, wheels extending like claws ready to catch him ... Then it's thundering overhead, so close he can see the rivets in its belly, smell the kerosene. The engine roar shakes his teeth. And a moment later it's gone over the chain-link fence, bouncing onto the runway half a kilometre downwind.

'Jesus Christ!'

'See?' says Carla, excited as a five-year-old. 'Isn't that amazing? Wasn't that worth it?'

She insists they wait for another one. They sit in the car and Smithy, still worked up, grabs a small bottle of spirits he keeps in the glove compartment. Carla's profile is outlined faintly by the city lights. Her skin swallows the light, only her eyes shining.

Smithy swigs, welcoming the fortifying trickle of fire into his belly.

'I wish you wouldn't,' she says, quietly.

'What?'

'Drink like that.'

Smithy keeps that smile pinned tightly to his face. 'Why? I'm not drunk.'

'I know, Danny. It's probably just me. I didn't tell you about my dad did I?'

Smithy shakes his head, casually screwing the lid back on the bottle, even though he'd dearly like another swig.

'He's an alcoholic, a gambling addict. He was violent towards my mom, but when I was young he didn't use to touch me. Then after Mom died I guess I was next in line. That was the main reason I worked so hard to get into college—just to get away from him.'

She starts to say something else, but just then another plane comes down over the car, obliterating her words. It slides down the windshield and he thinks of 9-11, the knife in America's fat white belly.

'How did your mother die?' he asks, to change the subject. The question seems safe enough, but she jerks like he's prodded her with a brand. 'Sorry, I ...'

'I told you, Danny! Breast cancer. Don't you remember? How the priest at my church tried to heal her? I told you all about it! That was why I lost my faith in God. I can't believe you don't remember that! And what you said made so much sense!'

To Smithy's horror she starts to cry, and Smithy tries not to panic. He was doing so well, and now two fuck-ups in quick succession are threatening to shatter the whole crystal palace of her illusions.

'Of course I remember.' He puts his hand soothingly on her thigh. 'And I meant what I said, okay? Do you remember what I said?'

She nods, choking on her sobs. 'About how our beliefs are like skins that we shed when we're ready ...'

'Yes ...'

She twines her fingers so tightly with his that it hurts. 'And even if we feel naked, that's just because we're not used to the new skin.'

'Uh, huh, that's right. You see? I remember.'

It's too dark to read her expression, but her eyes are wide and intense, searchlights scouring the darkness of his face for the gentle man she hopes he is.

'It's getting late, I'm tired. I wasn't thinking,' he soothes. 'Come on. Let me take you home.'

At her place he pulls up into a steep, cracked concrete driveway, jerking up the handbrake to hold the car on the incline. They sit in awkward silence, bathed in the cold light of the streetlights while the traffic swishes past on the road behind them. Smithy leans across the seat to kiss her, and the feel of her heavy lips is unfamiliar and somehow disturbing, the taste of her mouth different too. He puts his hands under her top. Her skin is oily and young and springy like rubber. He feels like he is bouncing off her, like there is another layer of clothing on her he can't get under. He presses a hand into the crotch of her jeans, trying to feel her flesh through the hard material, and they writhe together, colliding and refracting and shocked by the contact of their skins and the confrontation of such intimacy between strangers. Smithy fumbles with her bra strap, tries to reach her nipples.

'Wait,' she says. She breaks away. 'Wait. Can we go inside?'

He follows her up the steps to the house. She switches on the light in the living room, the jaundiced illumination of a low-watt bulb revealing a boxy old Sanyo TV in the corner, a dilapidated couch across which someone has cast a cheap imitation-batik print. Someone's takeaway containers on the floor. She takes his hand and leads him to her bedroom. It is small and airless. In the corner her bed; a thin single mattress on the floor, the bedclothes still tangled. Against the wall there's a small vanity on which she has arranged her beauty things: hairbrush, cosmetics, a few bits of jewellery. She snatches up a tampon wrapper from the floor, a bus ticket, an empty chewing gum packet. She sits nervously on the mattress and Smithy sits next to her.

'There's something you should know. I told you I wasn't very experienced, right?'

'That's okay.'

'No, but I mean, I'm ... I haven't ...'

Smithy stares at her.

'This is the first time, Danny.' The words come in a rush. 'I should have told you, I'm sorry, I know. But I want to. At least I think I do. It's just ... I don't know what I'm supposed to feel. Or do ...'

Smithy and his mates used to boast about laying virgins. The sly smirk: *Raised the Japanese flag on the weekend, mate. No bullshit.* It was bullshit, though. Of course it was. Now it's happening for real, but he doesn't feel like he thought he would. Still, she said she wants to.

He puts his hand on her leg and tries to slide it between her thighs like a letter-opener. 'It's easy,' he says. 'Just relax and I'll show you what to do.' But she keeps her legs scissored together.

'The church I used to be in was very strict about sex, very big on hell and sin and all that. And even though I don't believe it anymore, I still get their voices in my head, you know?'

'You hear voices?'

'No, no, nothing crazy or anything. Just the voices of the preacher or my mom or whoever. Voices of the church.'

'Saying what?'

She looks down, embarrassed.

'Saying what?'

'*The fornicators will burn in hell.* That type of thing. I know, it sounds mediaeval doesn't it? But I can't help it. I'm brainwashed.'

'Relax, Carla. You'll be fine.' He caresses her cheek. 'You trust me, don't you?'

She looks at him, and Smithy sees that close up she's not as pretty as he thought. Her skin is coarse with the pores of a recent adolescence, her cheeks a little puffy. 'I think so,' she says.

'You think so?'

She's about to answer when there's a buzzing in her handbag. She reaches for it.

'Don't!' Smithy yelps. It comes out loud, much too harsh.

She stops, looks at him.

'Just don't. Not now.'

'Okay...' She puts the bag back down again carefully. 'What do you want me to do?'

'Just lie down,' he says.

She does, stiffly, on her back like a toy soldier someone knocked over. Smithy gets up and goes back to switch off the light. Now it's pitch black except for a faint glow through the gauzy curtains that illuminates nothing. The girl breathes in the dark, and Smithy goes to her, lays down beside her. He can smell her sweat. There's not enough room, and he's half on the carpet. He puts out his hand and feels her there, the tight rise and fall of her belly.

'Danny?' Her voice is little and frightened, and he knows he should stop, but as his hand moves over her warm, yielding skin, he finds he can't anymore. He has her now, under his fingers: her breasts, her thighs, her neck beneath his fervid lips, her blackness in the blackness like a double negation, like an absence made flesh, and he's full of a great, morbid longing. He's swollen, aching, bursting with it. He finds the edge of her jeans, pops the button. The zip parts like a ripping fruit, and he slides his hand in deep, all the way to the pulp. He's devouring that incarnate darkness like a fire, and words—dirty, reckless words—are coming up that rusty pipe now whether he likes it or not, but he doesn't care. He's going to gush it all into her. At last, at last.

Then she seizes his wrist. 'Stop! Stop! Wait.'

'What? What is it?'

Smithy's heart pounds in the silence like a bass amp below the threshold of hearing. And then she says: 'I want to pick up that message.'

A cold rush of fear: she suspects. Both their bodies are frozen in position, poised in an electric stillness like two wild animals that have stumbled upon one another, in the moment before predator or prey explodes into action.

He tries to pull himself back to a place of control, to make his voice nice. 'Come on, Carla. Not now. I want to be with you.' He fumbles again between her legs, trying to arouse her.

'No! I want to see who it's from.' She wrenches his hand from her pants, twists her body away.

'No, Carla!' He tries to grab hold of her in the dark, manages to get his arms around her legs as she hauls herself to her feet.

'Let go of me!' She pushes him and he stumbles, disoriented in the alcoholic dark, falling forward and cracking his face hard against the edge of her dressing table. A stunned numbness and pain and a gush of warmth down his lip. The slick, rusty tang of blood. He clutches his face. 'Oh fuck! Oh Jesus! I think I've broken my nose!'

Carla's already across the room. She hits the light. Smithy is crouched on the floor holding his face, the blood running between the webs of his fingers. But she doesn't care. She has her phone out, she's looking at the screen. When she looks up again, her eyes are wide.

'Who ... who ...' she stammers. 'Who are you?'

Smithy stumbles to his feet. He comes towards her and she shrinks from him. In her eyes naked fear. And disgust, horror, revulsion. Her face is curdled and twisted with it.

'Greg,' he says, flatly, through the bloody mess of his nose. 'Greg Smith.'

Her eyes are wild with incomprehension. 'But, but ... who's that?'

He gives a mirthless snort. 'Nothing,' he says. 'Nobody. Don't worry about it.'

The front door is open, and the sound of the trucks comes through clear with the chilling air, and for just a moment Smithy is sure it's a dream: the staring girl and the taste of shock and the great whispering indifference of the city. He's standing in the same desolate dream that he's lived again and again, and he has the strangest sensation that something important comes next, that everything is stacked to collapse in some portentous way. The girl's lips are moving and starting to form words, and Smithy thinks maybe this is it—maybe she's going to tell me. Then he blinks and it's gone, and the girl is screaming and shrieking, like a wild thing, a crazy person, and nothing she's saying makes any sense at all.

Freak

My name is Michael Freck, but everyone calls me Freak. Not everyone, Johnno calls me Michael or sometimes Mick because he's a friend. I used to hate being called Freak. I still do but I've got used to it so it doesn't seem so bad anymore and sometimes I don't feel anything.

My little brother, Ari, also gets called Freak but it's worse when they call him that 'cos he can't speak and nobody knows why. He can make a noise but it sounds like a parrot or something. It's a squawk really, not words. All the kids think he's a retard but he's not. He's smarter than me and can do long division in his head. I stuff it up even when I've got a pen and paper. He can write too. He always has a little pad of sticky notes and a pen so that when he needs to say something he can write it down. Sometimes he writes really funny things but he's got a sick sense of humour and most of the time I'm the only person who gets it. Even Mum doesn't. Ari's got a round face. When Dad used to read us *The Faraway Tree* I knew that I was Joe and he was Moonface, even though Moonface isn't one of the kids. Even Johnno says that Ari is weird 'cos his face never changes so nobody can tell what he is thinking. But it does really, you just have to get used to it. It's kind of like looking at a rock, it doesn't really change but you can still see shadows and sun passing over it. I tried to explain this to Johnno but he said Mate, soon I'll be calling you Freak too if you don't shut up.

Ari and I are the only Jews at our school except for some other ones who you wouldn't know were Jewish 'cos they don't wear a yarmulke or eat kosher or anything. There's another school that's not even that far away where most of the kids are Jewish and I once told Mum that it would be better for Ari and me to go there, especially Ari 'cos he wouldn't be a freak in two ways, but only in one. But Mum said that's a private school and since Dad died she can't afford to send us there and stop asking me 'cos you know it upsets me. And Ari kept eating his breakfast without looking at us but I could tell he was really wishing she would say yes.

Before Dad died he bought a dog and called it Cerberus 'cos that's the name of a three-headed dog that guards hell. He bought it 'cos he said Mum would feel safer in the house at night when he passed away if there was a dog around. Mum said Cerberus was a stupid name and none of us ever called him that, but no-one could think of a better one so while we were waiting for someone to think of something we called him Dog. After a while every name started to seem like it didn't fit as well as Dog and so he got stuck with that.

Dad got Dog from a friend who worked as a security guard. He said he asked for a really fierce one but something must have gone wrong 'cos Dog is really pathetic even though he's an Alsatian. Dad put up a sign on the fence that says Beware of the Dog with a picture of this really scary Alsatian showing its teeth. Before Dad got too sick he tried to teach Dog to be a guard dog like the one on the sign but I don't think he was very good at training animals 'cos all they ever did was scramble around on the lawn with a rolled up newspaper, mucking around. And then Dad said that he didn't think Dog had any aptitude.

It wasn't long after that that Dad couldn't walk anymore, 'cos the tumour was pressing against his spine and cutting off the nerves. The funny thing was, there he was, just about dying and everything, but all he seemed to worry about was who was going to protect Mum and us kids when he wasn't around anymore. Mum used to always sigh and say it's not like it's the Bronx, but Dad would say you've got no idea, they hate us here.

He made Mum buy this really fancy alarm system, even though she said it was a waste of money and she hated having to put in the numbers. And then she'd forget all the time and the alarm would go off and Mrs Colosimo next door got so sick of it she stopped talking to us. Dad also wanted a new security door and a cyclone fence and a special button that would ring an alarm at the police station, but Mum said there wasn't enough money and it was hard enough putting food on the table right now. Dad made her promise to at least get the new security door when the money from his life insurance came through, and she said she would but she must have had her fingers crossed when she promised 'cos we still only have the old wooden door and Dad's been dead for ages.

Even though Dad was always muttering about how Dog had let him down, Dog loved Dad. He was always sitting with his head on Dad's feet and staring up at him in his wheelchair and Dad would get all cranky and tell him to stop being so doleful, it was depressing him, and curse Dog for being so soppy, when what he really wanted was an attack dog.

When Dad finally went into hospital for the last time, Dog got really depressed and didn't even want to go for runs anymore, which was really weird, 'cos before that runs were the only thing Dog ever wanted to do. Whenever he wanted to go for a run, he would go and get one of your running shoes and put it in front of you on the floor. Then when you took it, he'd go and get the other one. He always got the right shoe, except for the time when Ari hid all the matching shoes, then Dog was gone for ages, until he finally came back with a sandal. Dog wasn't much of a guard dog, but he was pretty smart.

When Dog got depressed, Ari used to go and sleep on the sofa with him, even though Mum said he wasn't allowed to. But every morning when we came in for breakfast, he'd be curled up on the sofa with his head on Dog's lap and Mum would get really cross and yell at him about getting fleas, and Ari would look at her with his stone face. Eventually Dog started letting Ari take him for walks again and, after that, everyone knew that Dog belonged to Ari. The thing was, after Dog's depression got better, Mum got depressed and started taking lots of pills. I didn't know why she took the pills 'cos they made her even more depressed. It was really yucky 'cos she'd talk funny like all the words were mashed up together and she let the house get really dirty, until Ari and I decided that we'd better do the cleaning from now on, even though we hate cleaning.

Then one night Mum asked Ari and me to go to the 7-Eleven to buy her some Panadol, and we'd bought the pills and we were walking through the shops on High Street when these two guys started yelling heil Hitler at us. I could tell Ari was scared 'cos his ears went a little bit red like they always do when he is scared and I said ignore them they're just idiots. Anyway people are always yelling dumb stuff like that at us so I wasn't worried. But when they started following us I felt a bit sick and I said run home Ari, and he tugged my sleeve 'cos he wanted me to run too but I wouldn't 'cos then they'd have got us both. So I yelled run at him again and he did.

Then they caught up with me and one of them was big and fat and the other was small and skinny and kept on hopping around like the footpath was so hot he couldn't stand still. They smelt of beer and the big one said where you going Jewboy, Auschwitz, and he thought that was really funny. Then he said what's that you got, and I didn't realise I was still holding the Panadol till he knocked it out of my hand and then he goes Panadol, you're gonna need more than that. And the skinny one said why don't you go home to where you came from and the fat one said yeah, why don't you go back to Iz-ray-el? I said I was an Australian and I didn't come from Israel and he hit me in the mouth and said don't answer back. I was surprised 'cos even though I could feel blood it didn't hurt at all. Then he grabbed my yarmulke and goes hey look Marto, the kid's wearing a Frisbee on his head and he threw it at him. The skinny one called Marto said I hope they serve kosher food at the hospital, and he looked at the fat one like he'd said something really funny but the fat one didn't laugh. He said lie on the ground and I didn't move so he shouted lie on the ground and so I did.

When I was starting to lie down, I said a prayer in my head even though the funny thing was I wasn't really scared anymore 'cos I knew I'd had it. I figured you must only stay scared as long as you think you might be able to get away. Then Marto kicked me in the head and it bounced around a bit but it still didn't hurt, so I started hoping that maybe none of it would hurt even if they killed me and then I'd only have to worry about the dying bit and not the pain.

Then I heard a squawk like a parrot and I knew that Ari had come back, and the fat one turned around and said well fuck me that other kid's come back—sorry about the swearing but that's what he said. When I heard Ari squawk I felt this tingling in my chest and I thought, that is love, and that was funny 'cos it was like it was the first time I'd ever seen it, a bit like how you hear about lions and see them on the TV and everything but then when you go to the zoo for the first time you still go wow, so that's a lion. I was surprised 'cos I'd never thought about loving my little brother before that. Then I started feeling scared again and I realised love isn't always good, 'cos when you know you are going to get hurt you can let go of caring but when it's someone you love who's going to get hurt you can't, which means as long as you love someone you can always get hurt in the world and there's nothing you can do about it.

Then the skinny one said hey he's got a dog and he sounded worried but the fat one goes big fucking deal and he kicked me between my legs. And this time it really, really hurt and I wanted to cry but I couldn't make any sound, just a really quiet croaking noise. I thought I wonder if this is what Ari feels like when he can't talk, just like something wants to come out and it keeps growing inside you but it never bursts, it just fills you up more and more with the pain of it. I suddenly realised I didn't know anything about what it's like to be the person who is closest to me in the world and that felt strange, but what seemed even stranger was having these thoughts while someone was beating me up in the middle of the footpath at night.

But it turned out to be a big mistake for the fat guy to kick me 'cos I saw Dog flying through the air and his teeth were out like white daggers. I couldn't believe it was Dog 'cos he looked like a real attack dog. And Dad would have been proud, the way he grabbed the fat guy's arm just like Inspector Rex on TV and the skinny one started saying fuck over and over and then ran away even though the fat one was screaming help get it off me. Ari was jumping up and down and squawking and he looked almost as fierce as Dog who was biting the man really hard and shaking his arm. Then Ari made a different noise and Dog let go and the man ran away but his arm looked pretty bad from what I could see.

When we got home Mum said oh my God what happened to you, Michael, who did this to you, you're a mess and why in God's name are you smiling? And I told her what had happened and she said good dog, good dog and she gave Dog a whole leg of lamb with the meat on it and everything and none of us could stop patting him and Dog wagged his tail a lot.

Then I said sorry I lost the Panadol and Mum started crying and I felt really bad, but then she cuddled me so hard it started to hurt a little bit and I realised she wasn't crying about the Panadol. Then she cuddled Ari too and she said can we be a family again which was weird 'cos I didn't know we had stopped, but I kind of knew what she meant and I said does that mean Ari and I don't have to do the vacuuming anymore?

Different Kinds of Heaven

Zoe came over to Mickey's house one evening in December, a bottle of red wine in her hand, and this memory would always stay with him: her liquid shape through the rippled glass as she stood on his doorstep, and then the physical impact of her as he opened the door: her long loose limbs, the clean smell coming off her damp hair while the cicadas shrilled in the balmy dark. When she kissed him he felt the tight stretch of her smile against his mouth, the wine bottle clink against the keys in his pocket. Their mouths parted and her body slid across his as she brushed past him into the hallway. She had come for the love they would make—tonight—and he followed her into the house feeling weightless and unreal.

She taught piano for a living, and ran ten kilometres a day. Her body contained the contradictions of a runner and a pianist. Or perhaps no contradiction after all: her metronomic feet ticking off the miles, the stairwell labour of scales. Grace, and discipline, and a certain lyricism in her movements. Was that it? There was some erotic trick to her he could never pin down. Was it the small mole beside her mouth, or the dark, almost severely straight hair, hair a girl could do nothing with, but which feathered and lashed his cheek when her weight fell on him on the bed? Or was it simpler than that? Was it just the way she fucked, abandoned and dirty and beautifully pornographic?

Mickey had a six-year-old daughter, May, whom his ex brought round every second weekend. He was getting to know her still, after the two and a half years when he and Cathy hadn't spoken. The only times he'd seen May during that time were through the window of his parked car, bleak vigils driven by a grief which glimpsing her only sharpened. Coming out of Cathy's place on a blustery winter afternoon in a duffle-coat that made her look like Paddington Bear, or going into the supermarket and emerging again half an hour later, skipping beside her plastic bag-laden mother. He'd watch the house for hours, nothing changing whatsoever except dark drawing in, while inside, his daughter's childhood was taking place.

Now at last he had these weekends, and found he didn't know what to do with her at all. The car door would slam in the street, and there she'd be at the end of the drive, with her overnight case in one hand and Puss-puss, her stuffed toy, dangling from the other. He'd open his arms, and while she came to him, his eye would be drawn to the dark head in the car, watching. The long pause before she turned the ignition and the car slid off.

This mistrust made him defiant, but still he had no idea. When he lifted her up and spun her round he half-expected his big dumb hands to be seared by contact with such loveliness. Mayflower, he said, kissing her cheeks. According to the scales she weighed fourteen kilograms, but he could not believe it. She felt light as a kite, only the pulsing imbalance of her kicking legs indicating she had any weight to her at all. What do you do when a butterfly lands on your shoulder? You hold your breath and wait and try not to move so you won't damage it.

But holding still, he knew, would not protect her from harm, this serious child whose wide brown eyes took in everything, like she was swallowing the world whole. He would need to act, to decide, to care and nurture, he knew this—but when it came to fathering he felt clueless, an actor cast without a script. He remembered the first day she came, standing in his empty living room—he'd cleaned and vacuumed for the occasion, thinking he was preparing for her, making an effort, but now as she stood there on the bare carpet, a sad but polite traveller, he understood he'd got it all wrong.

Zoe didn't seem to mind the alternating weekends: May, Zoe, May, Zoe, like seasons or something, rolling around too quickly. Zoe asked after May, but never pressed to meet her and he figured it was better that way, keeping things separate, another complication he wouldn't have to mess up.

In bed they talked music, or books. Zoe loved Milan Kundera. Told him how a boyfriend once gave her his collected works for her birthday. Not some special collected edition—he'd gone from second-hand bookshop to second-hand bookshop, painstakingly tracking them down for her. Then he gave them to her bound up in twine, with some lines of Pablo Neruda he'd copied out:

Leaning into the afternoons I cast my sad nets

Towards your oceanic eyes

For God's sake.

It was, she said, the best present she'd ever received.

Did you love him then? Mickey asked her, with a forced casualness.

No, no, she said, shaking her head. She hadn't ever really loved him. But still.

Her favourite was *The Book of Laughter and Forgetting*. So Mickey borrowed her copy and read it, devouring it one Sunday lying in the backyard on an ex-housemate's discarded mattress. He flipped over restlessly in the sun, reading the pages in the shadow of his hand, occasionally letting the book fall and closing his eyes, as dazzled by the ideas as by the sun pouring red gold through the blood of his eyelids. He found an inscription from her ex inside the front cover that brought a queasy stab of jealousy: *Let us laugh, but never forget.*

Zoe brought around ingredients for a stir-fry. He stood behind her watching her slender hands quickly floret the broccoli, gather up the pieces and throw them into the sizzling peanut oil. His stereo played random tracks from his collection. She wielded the knife with an efficient musicality, the same way her hands moved over the keyboard. He folded an arm lightly around her belly and rested his chin on her shoulder, feeling her smile against his cheek. She kept chopping the vegetables, and The Triffids' *Bury Me Deep in Love* swelled up from the player, a soundtrack for the moment so apt to his emotion he felt exposed, his embrace suddenly self-conscious. But she didn't shy away, she let him hold her through the song.

Love? No, she'd never loved anyone. Or only once, a man she couldn't have. It was always the same for her, the same hope and then disappointment. She'd told Mickey this the first morning she stayed over. He'd woken to rain, the tick of water on the sill, the window tree scraping the glass. And Zoe's long naked back, her private breathing. He ran his thumb down her spine, as if he was unzipping her skin. Still half-blurred by sleep, she rolled into him, and their bodies merged in the pale predawn in a blissful confusion of surfaces. Only slowly did sex sharpen the boundary between them, their coupling bodies seeming to arise out of the dozy haze of their caresses without any conscious thought, like a picture slowly coming into focus.

And then afterwards at some point, he murmured something in her ear and she laughed, and the spell of wordlessness broke. She got up for the toilet. Mickey watched the ceiling, the faint play of shadows as the tree outside surged and shivered in the wind—something lonely in the endless random motion. Against the other wall was May's bed—he couldn't afford a whole room just for her, so he'd bought her this little bed, its two sides shaped like bananas. There was still a little whirlpool of unmade sheets around the place she'd slept. Such was the awkward compression of his life these days.

When Zoe came back she was distant and started pulling on her clothes. What's wrong? he asked, putting a hand on her back.

Nothing.

Nothing's nothing.

And then, because he pressed her, she told him: how she never loved anyone, there was always this corrupting doubt.

Never? he asked, disbelieving. Never anyone?

She bit her lip: There was someone, but he doesn't count.

Mickey shook his head, not understanding.

Nothing ever happened. And he was married. He never loved me, but I think it flattered him that I was so ... obsessed with him. I was like a toy on a string for him, pushing, pulling. He would never cut me free, you know? And I couldn't do it for myself. I needed him to be cruel, but he never would. She clenched her fist.

Mickey watched her expression, trying to read it. Would she still come if this man called her?

Then she went, and her absence left a ringing imprint on the silent house. He got up and ate bacon and eggs and stared for a long time into the small patch of his garden, where the old mattress was soaking in rain. Washing his face in the bathroom, he noticed again the looseness of his jowls, the coarse grain of his cheeks, the springy white wires amid the black nest of his hair. Running a hand through it he smelled Zoe. She was stuck to his fingers like honey, caught in his pores. The scent of her body was all over him, wherever her nakedness had brushed. Such dumb luck that she was his, he thought. Yet the eyes in the mirror were sad.

Mayflower, he called her, for the corolla of blond hair that haloed her face. But this was not promising, since his pot plants never did well. He tried to guess if they wanted sun or water, and always seemed to jump the wrong way. As for May, he never knew what to cook for her. He found she'd eat bolognaise, so he made her that until one day she said,

I don't like bolognaise, and that was that. So he struck on the idea of fish-fingers—he felt absurdly pleased with the inspiration—and this kept him going for a while.

Entertainment was a bigger problem. He bought a huge box of Lego for her after the first disastrous weekend, but she was always demanding his participation. He could not understand why something as seemingly easy as playing with Lego people could be so exhausting. Fifteen minutes and he'd be unable to sit upright anymore; he'd slump to the floor beside her, utterly drained. He was in a Lego gulag. His suffering passed May by. Her Lego people cheerfully conquered the mountains of his chest, danced on the pinnacle of his nose. He let it wash over him. It was all okay so long as he didn't have to raise a muscle. And all this killed half an hour, then she would ask him, what now, Dad? and he really couldn't think of a thing. How on earth did Cathy make the hours pass?

He took her to the Collingwood Children's Farm, where for a time he thought he'd failed again, until he understood that this stillness, this sombre concentration, was her expression of rapture. She held the guinea pigs like a sacred responsibility. Then afterwards they walked along the Yarra in a fine wash of sunlight, past the serrated skyline of the old factories, the embankments of yellow sour subs. She picked the fattest ones and happily chomped their squeaky stems from the nub up, a childhood delicacy he remembered well, though the taste disgusted him when he had a nibble for old time's sake.

She chewed them thoughtfully and he could see she was puzzling something out. Then she said: What if I don't like heaven, Dad? I mean, when I die?

You will. Everyone likes heaven.

Are there different kinds of heaven for different people?

I don't know, sweetie. Maybe you get what you want. Maybe your heaven would be a garden with the hugest sour subs.

She walked silently for a while, studying the river, the people quietly whirring by on their bicycles. Then she said, cheerfully, definitively: My heaven would just be a normal life!

He knew what she meant: that this was enough, right here, right now, and she could foresee not a single shadow.

Oh, darling, he said, stopping to crouch and gather her into his coat, his sudden change of mood confusing her. This love was not fair, he thought. He'd been tricked. His own heart was armoured and weary, and protected because he considered himself disposable, not really so important. But loving her made a break in his defences through which pain could get in again, along with the light she brought. Against this weakness there was no possible protection.

He always knew the danger with Zoe. A woman who said she never loved, and who was he to change that? He had no weapons to make her love him. So he told himself to keep one foot out, to love her with half his heart if he absolutely had to love her. On the phone, in those conversations, she told him she was feeling anxious, that she enjoyed being with him, but as soon as they were apart she felt heavy, the weight of an undertow. It was exhausting, this wading against herself, this same old story of hers. I'll hurt you, she said. I hate the guilt of doing this. And he said that getting hurt was neither here nor there, when, if he had understood himself properly, what he meant was: Don't leave me yet.

So she came to his house one evening in December with a bottle of red wine in her hand, and Mickey realised he had fallen in love with her in spite of himself, there being no half-hearted love, and she stood in his living room, leaning back against the mantelpiece, breasts thrust out, sipping wine from a glass tulip.

I shouldn't be here, she said.

So you always say.

He put one hand on her breast and she took a gulp of wine.

Why do you always do that? she said.

What?

Why do you always touch me when I'm trying to tell you that ...

He didn't answer. He stepped against her body and she propped the wine glass on the mantelpiece, let her fingers entwine with his, their arms dangling between them like a chain. But her eyes fell.

Listen, he said.

To what?

Listen to the cicadas.

You're changing the subject, she said.

They live for a day.

Yes ...

They live for one day only.

Oh, Mickey.

They made love with King Kong playing on the computer on his desk. Dinosaurs tumbling in some endless chase scene while she opened for him, her sleepy-lidded cat eyes so close the whole time, her kisses wet on his face. He was buried in her body to the fingernails, the lips, the eyelids, and she came under him with a shudder, biting him and crying out. And all the time he was aware, in some corner of his mind, that she was not there, that he collided with her and did not touch her, that there was a crack in her cry that opened onto emptiness, and even when he held her breast in his palm, he was holding the outline of an absence, while all the time the real Zoe stood watching from the corner of the room, a little sad and still, and already turning away.

So he would not say, 'I love you.' He kept that for himself, though it was the hardest thing, finding a place still able to contain the words when everything else was just breath and light.

One last time. He was living for one last time. Every phone call took her further away, some inexorable cross-drift. He visited her at her place in Clifton Hill, a damp terrace house with cracked walls, a hallway smelling of mould. Her room was utter chaos, clothes and music and books and boxes piled up from wall to wall, the sheets of her bed unwashed and stiff. She sat on her bed and told him her life wasn't working and she didn't know why. She let him kiss her and laid back, lifting her hips for him to pull off her jeans.

Then one Saturday morning while May was playing with her Lego the doorbell rang. He opened and there she was in the bland winter light, her face as pale as the overcast sky. Her lips looked bloodless, her hair lank.

Can I come in? she said.

Umm, of course, he said, only realising he was still standing there barring her way when her face changed. I'm sorry, he muttered, and let her pass, confused by his own reluctance.

May, who was cheerfully prattling to herself as she manoeuvered a plastic pig around a maze, stopped when the door opened, looked up at the thin girl standing there, and for a moment Mickey saw Zoe as a stranger might: her youth with all its selfish troubles, wrapped up in that drab, grown-up coat. Just a girl, he thought, and felt something like shame, as if someone better than he were seeing him through May, judging.

Zoe, this is my daughter May. May, say hello to Zoe.

Hello, said the child sullenly, not liking anything about this.

Mickey I'm sorry, I didn't think …

It's okay. You should probably meet her I guess. He said it against all the evidence of his heart, and sure enough, she looked down.

Mickey I …

What? he said harshly.

She bit her lip, evaded his eye, squirmed. Like a child in trouble, he thought. For some reason he hated her for it. A vision flashed: his fist splitting her lip, blood on her teeth.

May was still playing with her pig, but quietly now, stiffly, as if the toy had become too heavy.

He took Zoe's wrist, drew her back into the hallway, closing the door behind them.

You came to say something. Say it then. He wanted to punish her by making her be cruel. Anything other than this childish guilt of hers.

She looked at him at last, her eyes pleading, and he felt a rush of savagery, a mess of love and hate. *Fuck you*, he mouthed, satisfied to see the tears loosened in her eyes. That's better.

She turned and walked out, not closing the door, and when he went back to his daughter he left it that way, the security door lightly banging on its hinges, the empty day spilling in, until finally May said she was cold, and he closed it for her.

Then he made the mistake of putting on some music, and of course The Triffids came on. It lanced his heart, he was completely undone, standing there amid the Lego rubble in front of the morning window. He was holding his face and sobbing and hot tears were leaking out of him like something bust in his head.

Dad? said May. Her face was full of worry and a thousand watts of pure love. He crouched down, a total mess, snot everywhere, and she came to him, face into his ear, and made a necklace of her arms. She was on her tip-toes and he was teetering on his heels and it was so absurd it made him snort with laughter through his tears, the imbalance in their sizes, as if her tiny frame could hold up his bearish bulk, the weight of so much life she could never understand. But the funny thing was she could. She held him and the white light of morning poured through his cracks and he could have died with the bliss of her, he could have died then and there.

Then he let her go, held her small body out at arm's length. Her face was a crumple of concern.

It's okay, he said, smiling. I'm okay.

She wriggled from his grasp.

Help me build a tower? she said.

Suburban Mystery

When he was sixteen, my best friend Adrian ran away from home. It must have been 1983, the year of the fires, because I remember standing in the heat of the backyard in that eerie roseate light, as a fine fleck of ash, white as a snowflake, drifted down to settle on my hair. The sun was a bronze coin smoking in the acrid sky, and the world was tinted a stained-glass cerise, as if tainted by the possibility of destruction.

Adrian's pale face surfaced in the black of my bedroom window one midnight. He was hungry so I stole food for him from the pantry: apples, dried apricots, Salada biscuits and peanut butter. Stuffed them up my jumper and brought them out to him where he was sheltering in the shell of the half-built house next door. It was exciting, a clandestine mission like in the days when we'd gone on unauthorised adventures in Grade Six, our 'iron rations' wrapped in a tea-towel on a stick, the cartoon-approved and only way to go AWOL.

We sat up on the second storey and he crouched there like some kind of bird, his bony knees poking through the holes in his jeans, while he wolfed down the food. He had an Adidas bag in which he carried his worldly possessions: a change of clothes, a copy of *Catch-22*, his Bauhaus and Joy Division records, a packet of Peter Jackson super mild, and two bottles of red wine. I went back into enemy territory to fetch a corkscrew and a blanket.

I got drunk for the first time up there in that empty space full of echoes and moonlight and scraps of electrical wiring. I suggested an experiment.

We would see to what extent it was possible to mentally resist the effects of alcohol. I'd read books and I believed the mind could do anything. I forced down gulp after gulp of the cold wine until my face went numb and my words slurred. The moonlight sloshed over us and I sprawled out on the bare floor and watched the trees through the window spin without ever completing a rotation. The wine bottle got knocked over and glugged out a great purple stain.

'Where will you go?' I asked him.

'I dunno, I don't care,' he said. His cigarette end dived and darted like a firefly. He'd been saying that a lot, about not caring. He didn't care about school, about the future, about his mum and dad. What was to care about? Nuclear war was bound to come sooner or later. We'd been expecting it for years. When we were younger we'd made plans to bury tins of food up on the Black Spur. We'd have mountain bikes and leave food on the doorsteps of people with less foresight than ourselves. Even at sixteen we still thought a little wistfully about the possibility of nuclear holocaust. At least it would be dramatic.

He opened the second bottle and I guzzled straight from the neck. Yes, hell, who cared? Through the window I could see the house I'd grown up in. It was as familiar as a face, like a big square head with windows for eyes, a head full of memories. But the last lights had gone out, its lids were drawn down. It slept unaware that I was out in the construction site next door, watching it with cold, unsympathetic eyes.

Adrian held up his hand, fingers outstretched. 'How many fingers am I holding up?' That was our ritual *Catch-22* gag—*I see everything twice*—a sort of comic antiphony in which the response was always 'two'. But I really was seeing double, and trying to focus on his hand caused a swell of nausea that sent me reeling down into the garden to barf a fumy, mulberry slurry into the grass outside my bedroom window. I rolled out on my back on the lawn, the world heaving under me like an anchorless ship and the trees surging in the wind like seaweed. Adrian came down and we vomited together in solidarity, our messes mingling in the grass.

Oh, that long, boring year! Bob Hawke's larrikin drawl on the radio after the America's Cup win, having a go at the wowser bosses, and Men at Work's vegemite sandwich song on every bloody radio. We despised it all. We slouched about outside the milk bar—archetypal teenagers with cigarettes and Samboy chips, slagging off parents, teachers and the world we didn't understand. We nicked gin from over the neighbour's fence and drank it at lunch time. Fucking revolting, we agreed. Like drinking perfume, we protested. And passed the bottle again.

That summer I bought my first record, *The Blurred Crusade* by The Church. As I slipped it out of its sleeve onto the turntable for the first time, the light caught a line of handwriting—some impenetrable in-joke —inscribed in the smooth black vinyl inside the last song. That opaque, mystic scribble fascinated me: Steve Kilbey's last elliptical utterance before the stylus spiralled into the black hole at the centre of the record. 'Almost With You' was my anthem. Its lush, anguished paisley-poetry made my soul bleed. When Steve Kilbey asked *Can you taste their lonely arrogance?* I wanted to shout: 'Yes, yes, I can.' I understood nothing he said, but I could almost not bear the sorrow and longing when he sang, *I'm almost with you, I can sense it wait for me. I'm almost with you. Is this the taste of victory?*

Adrian was sleeping rough, in concrete dust and bent nails, or in beds in youth homeless shelters, or under bridges, his own half-asleep dreams of approaching gangs, of boots and fists, pulling him back again and again to the interminable passage of the night. I watched him slip into the under-society of lost kids with white, white skin and unwashed clothes and mouths foul with cigarettes and swear words. They taught him how to inhale Preen from a plastic bag and break into a school by dismantling the slatted windows on the roof. I was afraid that he was slipping out of my orbit, heading for places I would be unable to follow.

But I wasn't sure I could grow up on my own. He'd been my best friend since kindergarten.

Adrian was a smart kid, always top of the class in maths. But he'd started failing and then he dropped out of school altogether. Still, I used to see him at lunch times quite a bit. He was bored shitless, so he used to come down to the park near the school with his girlfriend Kelly who, it turned out, was doing twenty valium a day. She liked to share them around like Smarties. If Adrian didn't care anymore, she cared even less. She chromed Mortein.

Tony Dawes used to hang out there too, a small twitchy kid we'd known since primary school. We'd watch him pashing his size-sixteen girlfriend against the fence, their mismatched pelvises pulsing together in a sort of obscene peristalsis. There was something going wrong in his head, though we didn't think too much about it at the time. When he wasn't having dry sex with his girlfriend, he was raving haywired about the monos and how they were coming. He never explained who they were, those awful monos, but we could see his terror of them. His eyes would rove randomly as he spoke, sliding again and again to the alley across the street, as if at any moment it would fill with daleks. When life was particularly dull, and we felt like passing the kicks down the pecking order, we'd stuff grass clippings down his shirt or punch his skinny shoulders. Time oozed by, Tony's muted shouts of protest falling dead in the heat.

Adrian smoked and rocked idly on the swings. He had adopted a certain way of crossing his thin, stove-piped legs, his forearm resting on his thigh in an arty manner he'd picked up from a Bauhaus album cover. In his all-black gear, his threadbare jeans, he was both crow and scarecrow. He smoked his nervous cigarettes and picked at people with the beak of his words until the stuffing began to come out of them. We all did. That was the thing we did, the way we were. It was peck or be pecked. We were miserable, inured, bonded by the gravitational collapse of our self-esteems.

Adrian pinched a shopping trolley from Safeways and we rode about in the thing like six-year-olds. Then he took it to the top of the infamous Melaleuca Street hill and jumped in. 'Don't be an idiot,' I told him, but he pushed off and it rolled away down the hill. Its trajectory was doomed from the start, anyone could see that. It wasn't made for those speeds, and halfway down the hill the front wheel buckled and it crashed onto its side and sent him flailing across the tarmac. Just then a car turned onto the street at the bottom of the hill. Adrian limped off the road and it went slowly past, the driver pausing to wind down the window and say something, to which he responded with a barked, hurting obscenity. By the time he got to the top of the hill he was laughing again, though his sleeve was sticky with blood and his wrist was swollen up like a balloon.

Sometimes those suburban streets took on a surreal aspect to me. All those damn orange houses, all those driveways, evidence of some kind of life, but more often than not you saw nobody at all. Maybe some old guy in a singlet watering his roses with a hose, nameless faces like that guy in the car on Melaleuca Street. The thud of a football kicked on an oval, coming late over the distance. There was something weird and mysterious about all this, it seemed to me. Who were the people all this belonged to? Are we happy here or not? Nobody was saying. Everything was sealed up inside those silent brick boxes, like the energy in plutonium, $e=mc^2$. We couldn't puzzle out the equation of our own hearts let alone of so many other atomic units, nuclear families. So can you blame us for carrying textas in our pockets, for making some kind of mark, however crass or banal, on that sealed-up surface?

We sought out high places, places that gave us some kind of perspective, like the overpass on the freeway where the wind stinking of exhaust blew hot on our faces. It was a good place to watch the night come in. The city in the distance glittered and took on a sci-fi aspect: crystalline towers, and the lights speeding below us, red and white, shaking the concrete pillars of the bridge. The air cooled and there was a softness about the violet sky, a beauty even in that hard, noisy place.

One night Adrian climbed up on the railing, and standing up there on a high wire above the city's streaming artery, closed his eyes and held out his arms as if trying to capture everything, the whole incomprehensible thing, inside his embrace. I was terrified. I wrapped my arms around his shins and pleaded with him, my face pressed into the denim. 'Please no, please stop it, come down.' He teetered, then his legs folded in my arms and he slid down my chest onto the concrete walkway. I broke down and wept, filled with shame but unable to hold in the great tearing sobs. My eyes shut tight against the hot flood, my hands over my face, I don't know what I saw there in the dark of myself.

'It's so strange,' he said.

I looked at his fierce face shining in the freeway lights.

He clenched his fist and then opened it as if letting something small fall to the ground. 'It's so strange and so ... fucking banal.'

Tony Dawes cut his wrists in the senior school corridor, leaning against the wall with a Stanley knife. Afterwards he stood there so quietly, unobtrusive as ever, that it took a while before anyone noticed his crimson gloves and the drip drip drip on the lino, the bloody footprint smear as kids rushed to class. The monos had arrived and he cut his wrists to get away from those crazy fuckers, but they came and got him anyway, poor bastard.

And one evening Adrian and I threw a coat-hanger across the powerlines on the street that bordered the school, shorting out a substation with a deafening bang and a fireball so bright we were temporarily blinded. For a few seconds we staggered about in darkness, hands groping in front of us, terrified that we had finally done something irrevocable, had lured the demons of brilliance and power from their hiding place and been struck blind for our hubris. Then the swimming blackness cleared to reveal the grass of the nature strip where I had fallen on my knees. The substation was on fire and half the suburb was blacked out. We got up and ran for it, awe and terror beating in our ears, but the houses stayed quiet as ever, nobody gave chase. I cannot remember where we ran or what we did afterwards. Outside of the illumination of that fireball, everything is dark now. I watch us run down the street, the sound of our footfalls fading in the humid twilight, while the substation buzzes and sparks and finally burns out cold.

Adrian went back to school and finished his HSC two years after me, got into IT and now works on an automated share trading system for a hedge fund. We met just the other day after work, got blind drunk, and made extravagant promises to chuck in our ethically suspect jobs the following Monday. For just a moment I really believed I could find the courage to do it. It's resignation, or resignation! I shouted at the woman next to me, who moved away to another table.

I'm married and living in a nice brick veneer house not all that far from where I grew up. We're extending this spring to make room for our third child—we're hoping for a girl this time. I drink too much, it's true, but other than that I've got a grip, you know? I've settled. I love and worry about my boys and I drink and I try to keep my marriage going, not that it's so bad, no worse than anyone's for all I know. I don't find any mystery in the houses on my street, or, to tell the truth, in anything much. I have, like most people, an almost evangelical belief in the ordinary.

But some nights I wake at four a.m. with the resonance of a frightening dream ringing in the silent bedroom. I am sinking in the harbour in concrete shoes, or I reach a black river and soldiers come to demand my fare, but my pockets are empty. My heart pounds but I cannot puzzle out the meaning, or is it just impossible to allow it in, as one cannot hold onto a burning coin? I get up and pad through the house to the bathroom and splash my face with cold water to drive away the dread. In the unforgiving glare I am shocked at the fine cobweb of age spreading over the face in the mirror, and wonder how the answers always seem to run ahead of me. Nothing has been solved, I realise, and the times I think it has been are an illusion, the lie of the banal that covers over an unknowable truth. I remember Adrian standing on the overpass and shaking his fist. So strange, and so fucking banal. And then I go back shivering to my bed and slide in next to my wife, sealed up and alone in the breathing envelope of her skin.

Angela's Parrots

It's a bleary winter morning and Angela is feeding the parrots. Doug stands at the kitchen window, watching her from behind the overcast glare on the panes while the toaster ticks. He notices her bare feet on the cold bird-shitty floor of the aviary and the shard of anger that lives in his belly twists. How hard could it be to put on a pair of slippers? Her toes look blue. She reaches into the plastic bag at her feet and pulls out two handfuls of seeds. The parrots swarm down for the food, covering her arms like flame.

The toaster bungs and spits his toast out onto the kitchen bench, having burnt it as usual. He swears and goes to work scraping the charcoal into the sink with a butter knife. When he looks up again, Angela is still standing in the same pose, arms out like the wings of an oil-slicked cormorant, staring unseeingly through the fouled wires of the cage. Her morning hair is mussed and unwashed. The gaudy birds claw and fight on her wrists, scratching her skin. 'Oh, for fuck's sake,' he swears. He scours the toast so hard it breaks in half and falls into the detergent suds at the bottom of the sink. Disgusted, he chucks both pieces in the bin and pours himself a bowl of cornflakes instead.

He eats the cereal without tasting it, thinking about Angela's performance in the aviary, her arms outstretched, Jesus-like, the blood-red splash of the parrots on her hands. They're both from Catholic families—it doesn't take much to trigger the familiar guilt that lies buried in his guts. His cornflakes go down to join the queasy mush of his insides. When he takes the bowl to the sink, Angela has finished feeding the birds. With her index finger she is stroking the yellow skull of her favourite parrot, Sunshine. Never was an animal more inaptly named, for Sunshine is a psycho-bird, a killer. Only Angela can go near it, and it has even drawn her blood on one or two occasions. Yet there she is, caressing its vicious little head with a sorrowful tenderness, staring out past the vegie patch, the fence, towards the pylons and the dull empty sky. Oh, Christ, he thinks, leave off with the poor caged bird thing. The bird rubs itself against her finger with half-closed eyes, then quite without warning bites her. She pulls back her hand and snaps, taking a swipe at the ungrateful creature. It flutters up out of reach and starts to shriek like a burglar alarm. White hands cover her face.

He flicks the switch on the electric jug and goes back to sit at the table. After a while the door opens and she comes in. Her bare feet leave muddy traces on the white tiles.

'Door,' he says.

She ignores him, going to the sink to blast hot water over her cold fingers.

'Door,' he repeats, with emphasis. Warmth is draining from the kitchen like blood from a well-stabbed corpse.

'What's the matter with you?' she says in the cold, distrait voice that drives him crazy. 'Why can't you ever remember to clean out the sink after you scrape your toast?'

'I was going to. Now would you shut the bloody door? It's friggin' freezing.'

'I'm warming my hands,' she explodes, as if this is the last straw. Then she crosses to slam the door shut, her hands dripping on the floor as she goes.

She drops her bread into the toaster, and he sits there sipping his tea and staring into indefinite space. Soon smoke begins to stream out of the toaster and it ejects her toast, suitably ruined. She butters the charcoal and eats it with a pained expression, the tendons in her neck straining as she swallows. He slams down his cup.

'What?'

He looks at her witheringly.

'What?'

He shakes his head. 'Never mind.' He goes to the sink and swills it clean.

Having swallowed the last of her burnt toast Angela gets up and disappears into the living room. He hears her pick up her guitar and strum a chord. For the past three weeks it's been the same: some Joan Armatrading song in A minor that sets his teeth on edge. A minor: that miserable, rainy day chord, that dreary three-finger pinch. All her own songs are written in it too. No matter what other tonalities she may experiment with, it is to A minor her fingers will return, like flightless birds unable to escape the pull of gravity. After a few strums her voice wavers into song, and he can't take it anymore. He walks out the front door and into the greasy light of day.

On a train between Hyderabad and Delhi, Doug struggles out of a viscous, claustrophobic sleep. With a jolt of panic he gropes for his money belt, but it's still there, unopened. How long has he slept? He looks through the bars on the window, but nothing about the barren, over-exposed plain gives him any indication of progress. The same sari-clad women lead the same buffalos along the side of the railway track. Despite the lulling rattle of the train, he feels suspended in place and time. An exhausting flatness and a permanent high noon brilliance that stabs his optic nerve. He is surprised to notice that his compartment is empty. When he fell asleep there had been four others in there with him. He gets up unsteadily, still dazed with sleep and heat, and makes his way along the carriage.

Three compartments along, he discovers why his own compartment is empty. Fifteen sweating Indian men are crammed into the space, along with a pretty western girl in a short denim skirt and a figure-hugging halter-top. The heat of the bodies and the stench of sweat is unbearable. The girl cowers against the window, staring resolutely through the bars while the men vacantly watch her tits.

Doug sees red. 'Okay, guys, enough already. Come on, back to your seats.' Fifteen pairs of insolently uncomprehending eyes swivel in his direction. 'Come on, shove off now. Leave the poor girl alone.' He makes herding gestures with his arms, but nobody moves, so he grabs the two nearest men by the arms and propels them along the train into the empty compartment next door. They expostulate busily in Hindi but don't resist. His arms are at least twice as thick as theirs. He comes back and grabs two more. They shake him off angrily, but get up and move down the train muttering under their breaths and shooting him looks of offended dignity. When he's all but cleared the compartment, he slumps onto the seat opposite the girl. She smiles at him. 'Hey, thanks for that. They're so brazen, it's unbelievable.' Her accent is all Aussie.

'Doug,' he says, offering her his big, freckled hand.

'Hi. I'm Angela.'

'You been here long?'

'Just flew from Melbourne last week. You?' She flicks a damp lock out of her eyes.

'Almost six months. Visa's up in a week. Hey, can I give you a tip—as an old hand?'

'Sure.'

'Go buy yourself some Indian clothes. Look I don't want to tell you what to do—I mean a lot of girls go around India dressed like you out of some kind of defiance, or feminism or something, but they could save themselves a whole lot of hassle if they just … adapted to the culture a bit.'

'What's wrong with what I'm wearing?' she asks innocently.

'Nothing—in Australia. But here, you might as well hang out a red light on your backpack. I mean, they just assume from the way you're dressed that you're as good as a prostitute. They can't imagine any other explanation for dressing so revealingly.'

She reddens. 'Oh my God.'

He eases back in the seat with a broad grin. 'Yeah, oh my God.'

One week before he has to leave the country—it's not much and they know it. No time to waste. In a little hotel room in Delhi he peels off the halter-top and stoops to taste the salt on her breasts. They make love in the wash of street noise that floats through the open window along with a mix of diesel fumes and incense. Machine-gun rapid Hindi, the belch of buses and the incessantly beeping rickshaws. His big hands open her up like a tangerine and the ceiling fan turns lazily above her upturned, pleasure-blind eyes. They lie on their sides on the single bed, arms tangled, their lips inches apart.

'It's only three months, then I'll be back in Melbourne.' Her lips smile, her eyes are sad. He kisses her.

The day before he has to fly out they hire a guide and make a trip out to the Old City. The crenellated sandstone wall encloses a seething human beehive. They feel an irrelevant guilt as the rickshaw-wallah—a man who might be in his sixties—pulls them through the streets. His muscles are strung tighter than wires. Sometimes a truck or a motorised rickshaw overtakes him and blurts a gout of exhaust in his face. The grime is so ingrained in his skin he seems part of the street itself, like a gutter or the underbelly of a bus.

Later, their guide grabs their hands and drags them down an alleyway. The stink of excrement is so overwhelming they have to hold their noses. But then he leads them down another lane and through an archway into a beautiful courtyard. Water tumbles from an ancient fountain and the intoxicating fragrance of sandalwood—the exact smell of a lover's body—fills the air. Plants of impossible verdancy shimmer in the cool. And while they stand there laughing with astonished enchantment, three huge, fabulously brilliant parrots descend out of the blue square of sky and alight upon Angela's shoulders and hair. She cries out in fear and delight, spreading her hands and shivering at the extraordinary sensation of their claws.

Their guide capers and his face splits into a grin full of gaps and betel-stained stumps. 'Oh, very good luck for the lady. Very very good.' Angela's eyes shine wet, and the guide goes on congratulating her and wobbling his head. 'Yes, yes …'

Finally he puts out his hand and says something, and the parrots hop onto his wrist. Their heads bob in comical mimicry of the little guide and one of them blurts a Hindi phrase.

'He is saying you *bahut sundar* … very beautiful … very beautiful lady, yes.'

The parrot nods and repeats: *Bahut sundar.*

The guide stands there oddly, hopping from foot to foot until they suddenly get it, and Doug fishes in his pocket for the baksheesh.

'Oh, thank you, sir. You are too generous.' And he leads them back into the alley and the stink of shit.

Back at the hotel she is still a little starry. 'Doug, they came to me.'

'Yeah,' he grunts. He knows, but doesn't say it: a tourist trick repeated ten times a day.

'That was amazing.'

And then because he doesn't want to hear more he seals her mouth with his.

Doug is lying on the border of sleep. The abysses begin to open between the joins of thought. He slides down and he's hearing the song. He's standing in the hallway and hearing her singing the words he's heard fifty, a hundred times. *This old love has me bound, but the new love cuts deep.*

He jerks awake. Stone cold awake. He shakes her shoulder, hard, till she surfaces.

'What?' The coldness in her voice.

'Who is he?'

'Who …'

Quietly. 'Who the fuck is he?'

The digital clock says 12:35. The five changes to a six. Then a seven.

'Gary.'

'Gary, the … the … industrial chemist? The paint bloke?' His voice drips with incredulity.

'He loves me in a way that …'

'DON'T.' He holds up his hand. 'Don't say it.'

'I'll say whatever I damn well …' His fists ball and go to his face and she shuts up. Her knee-jerk defiance is so stupid, so unbearably hollow he wants to punch her for it. More than for her infidelity.

Words, questions, protests leap inside him like fish in the dark. But in the end they subside into the general apathy of pointlessness that is filling him, and he just nods. 'Okay … okay.' He gets up and goes to sit in the kitchen in his jocks, shivering.

The full moon is a clock-face shorn of hands. It ticks across the space between the roof and the aviary, measuring the silence like a protractor.

When it's finally sunk, and the first pale blush of dawn greys the yard, he opens the door and steps out into the cold. Mud oozes between his toes as he crosses the garden. The earliest birds are beginning to sing in the black trees. In the aviary, the parrots are asleep with their heads under their wings, and they are startled and sluggish as he begins to haul them out and throw them clumsily into the air. They flurry briefly before settling back on the outside of the cage. Even Sunshine is too sleepy to attack him.

He swings his arms. 'Go on, you little fuckers. Fly. You're free.' They hop about and squawk weakly as he flaps at them.

Later, when Angela gets up to find the house empty, they'll still be sitting there on the filthy roof of their cage, waiting to be let back in. Only Sunshine will have taken his chance. He'll go hopping through the branches of trees just out of her reach, his eyes inscrutable beads, greeting the new day with his shrieking paranoid siren.

Growing Sickness

Something was eating Rufus Hamlin. His marks had taken a dive, his tenuous social life had withered to nil. He'd taken to reading Plath and Hemingway, and on the rare occasions he spoke, it was in ominously vague and philosophical terms, as if the concrete world could no longer touch him, or at the very least as if he didn't wish to be pinned down to the intelligible. His mother Denise—concerned because she herself had once suffered in the grip of a crippling depression—had sent him to a hypnotist, a psychiatrist, an acupuncturist, a chakra aligner and a Tibetan bowl practitioner, but the result was always the same: after three exhausting sessions trying to prise open that impenetrable mollusc of an adolescent, they would send him home certified either cured or incurable. Only the psychiatrist had wanted to keep him for further study. Rufus, he told Denise, had a severe Psychosexual Neurosis and needed long-term analysis if any hope was to be held for a normal adjustment.

It was certainly true that on anything to do with the subject of girls, Rufus was vastly and hopelessly confused. Perhaps it was fortunate that the psychiatrist never managed to gain a purchase on one of the roots of Rufus's problems, for if he had, he would have found it attached to so many others, in a network like the couch grass that had strangled the Hamlins' backyard, that he'd have been more or less obliged to pull up the entire intractable tangle and start again. One such root was the time when the nine-year-old Rufus had sneaked into his father's 'den' looking for something to play with and instead stumbled on a collection of pornography in a desk drawer. It was nasty stuff. Every page brought some new permutation of obscenity, revelations every bit as traumatic to the sensitive child's psyche as decapitation or dismemberment would have been. Why did his father possess such filth? The answer was obvious: it was a professional thing, research of some kind. Rufus had on a few occasions glimpsed parts of his father's slide collection of skin diseases and deep in his psyche the images converged: pornography and disease, bulbous goitres and swollen phalluses, pus and semen—all merged into a hellish tableau of carnality and disease, Hieronymus Bosch in porno pink.

In truth, however, the whole issue of sex was rather by the by, since Rufus was dying of cancer anyway. It had begun as a melanoma on his back that had metastasised and spread throughout his body. He'd sit in chemistry class and finger the lumps in his neck and weigh up the merits of bothering to pay attention to the ins and outs of the Haber process, given his likely lifespan. On the one hand he didn't want to let his parents down if he did survive as far as the exams. On the other, what was the point of doing all that work if he died before November?

Rufus considered it one of life's ironies that he was going to die of a skin disease when his father was the renowned skin specialist Henry Hamlin, author of the seminal *Hamlin Encyclopaedia of Dermatology*. In fact, one of the images that had wormed its way into Rufus's psyche when he'd sneaked a look into his father's slide collection was that of a young melanoma victim. His arm was raised to show how the disease had multiplied, black bubbles rising to the surface everywhere, like the cancer was boiling him to death from the inside. And to think that was what he'd be looking like not so long from now.

In the end, of course, someone would have to find out. Perhaps it would happen at dinner: his mother would lean across the table and say, 'What's that you've got on your neck?' And he'd pull up his collar and say, 'Nothing.' Then she'd insist on taking a closer look and discover not one, but a whole colony of sinister black mushrooms sprouting there. His father would go grey and make him take off his shirt and his mother would faint clean away at the sight of the hideous polyps blossoming all over his pale young body. Needless to say, with this awful secret, Rufus had never let a girl touch him, and he planned to keep it that way, not that anyone was applying.

Rufus's mother taught at a posh girls' school in one of those inner-south suburbs populated by blond women with orange skins and highly-strung temperaments, where the streets smell perpetually of Chanel N° 5. But she was not fooled by her charges' affluence and dazzling dental health. Having herself attempted suicide once in the distant past, she was well attuned to the ennui and hidden despair of these leafy, four-wheel-drive-infested suburbs. It was just fortunate for her that she was married to a doctor who had known what to do when he found her gargling vomit and half-dissolved barbiturates in the bed where she'd been spending most of the summer. Thankfully she no longer suffered from her suicidal episodes (except on rare occasions such as when someone made the mistake of criticising her cooking) and had in fact, by virtue of overcoming her demons, achieved an exemplary mental balance and wisdom. As a result she had become the de facto school counsellor ('call me Denise, dear'), and had adopted a number of troubled young girls for salvation.

Among Denise's favourite lame ducks (this being the light-hearted term she employed) was a girl by the name of Janis Mitchell, whom she had found in the girls' toilets, fist in mouth, tickling her own epiglottis. On the outside Janis was a lively, reckless redhead with a sensual, pretty-plain face, froggish but not without a certain freckled sex appeal. On the inside she was a black hole. Janis's mother was a bona fide sadist who had meted out her cruelty in tiny doses of criticism and disparagement which individually appeared almost innocuous—even salutary, corrective—but which, taken collectively over seventeen years, had proved sufficiently corrosive to completely dissolve the bedrock of her daughter's self-esteem. In place of a body image, Janis was left with a sort of giant nagging ulcer. Bulimia (she was astonished when she found out there was a word for it) was her personal brainwave, the bargain she'd struck between the opposed demons of craving and criticism that ruled her psyche.

Food was not the only way Janis attempted to fill the black hole that yawned in her innards. She also used men, or, as she collectively referred to them, dicks. Once she had sex with three randomly selected males from the Inflation nightclub, thus fulfilling her fantasy of having every hole simultaneously plugged, but the effect was not what she'd hoped. To cope with the ensuing emptiness she ordered in enough pizza and cake to feed Stalingrad. That Roman-scale debauch should finally have proved to her that that way lay madness. Yet the lesson left her none the wiser. The black hole was undiminished, and she could still only think of two physical methods of stuffing it.

Rufus, Janis. Janis, Rufus.

Janis and her mother had had their final falling-out, convulsions of mutual venom that ended with Janis marooned on the Maroondah with a pitiful bag of belongings she'd thrown together before quitting the viper's nest for good. She called Denise from a phone booth in hysterics, swearing she was going to throw herself in front of the next furniture truck—that would make the effing bitch sorry. So Denise—exhilarated by her own internal fanfare of drama and benevolence—drove out to where the poor girl was waiting, weeping and dishevelled on the grassy strip between a service road and the highway.

'Janis is going to be staying in the spare room for a while. Just until the end of the exams. Try to be friendly,' she told Rufus.

'Yes, Mum.'

'Hi!' The weird-looking redhead smiled at him, revealing teeth ruined by the repetitive action of digestive acids.

Rufus muttered something that sounded suspiciously like 'kill me now' and slouched off.

In Rufus's semi-conscious association Janis was Janis Joplin, the suicidal redhead who would never ride through Paris in a sports car with the wild wind in her hair. Or was Janis the one who would ride through Paris, and in fact it was his mother Denise who, at the age of thirty-seven… It was a bit muddled. Anyway, his mother had always been a fan of the hoarse-voiced rocker who famously gave Leonard Cohen head on the unmade bed of the Chelsea Hotel, and now she'd adopted this little Aussie namesake/lookalike, as if keeping her own unexpressed wildness as a pet. But much as she might have derived a vicarious thrill from Janis's devil-may-care exploits (Janis told her everything), she let the girl know in no uncertain terms she must never touch her boys, by which she meant husband or son. Janis looked truly shocked and abashed at this admonition. Such a thought had never occurred to her!

In any case Janis was not Rufus's type. Rufus was desperately in love with Fiona Doherty, Fiona Elkowitz and Fiona Byrd, the dreaded 'three Fionas' of the high school he attended. Oh Fiona, he'd groan in onanistic morning reveries, as the hallucinated triumvirate flickered over his aching body, their fickle interchangeability frustrating his attempts to imbue the fantasy with an illusion of solidity. All three were fantastically good-looking and wildly out of reach, which was exactly what a boy like Rufus was after: ethereal vessels into which he could pour his wasted seed without the slightest risk of consummation. His visions were soft-core, indistinct, pointedly un-lurid.

Janis was supposed to be saving her final school year under Denise's tutelage and guidance, but the truth was she'd written the year off and only kept up the pretence of study for fear of being cast out by her new guardian if she didn't. As soon as Denise was out of the house, she'd head to the fridge to struggle with the question of how much ice-cream would not be missed, or flop disconsolately into the bean bag in Rufus's room and try to distract him while he worked on programming his computer adventure game. This he found intensely irritating since lately it had taken an erotic twist involving water-nymph versions of the three Fionas, and he couldn't work on the code with her in the room.

'I miss my Dougy!' she sighed once.

Rufus's attention did not waver from the lines of gibberish on the screen: 'Is that your boyfriend or something?'

'What? No! What type of a name is Doggy?'

'Oh, I thought you said Dougy. *If y is greater than x then input …* Hold on, that's not right!'

'You know what I did to him once when I was bored?'

'This doesn't make sense [slamming the delete key]. What? No, don't tell me.'

'It was only once!'

He finally looked at her. 'You … touched the lipstick?'

'He's a cocker spaniel.'

'A whata … ? You're disgusting!'

Or another time: 'Aren't you interested in girls, Rufus?'

'I'm not gay if that's what you're getting at.'

'Because if your mum hadn't told me to leave you alone I might even like you. You're quite cute you know.'

This was patent rubbish. He was the most inadequate, hideous, weasly specimen of a male as it was possible to conceive of. Furthermore, he had terminal cancer, which was right now swelling like little black cauliflowers inside and out. He was a doomed, festering carbuncle of a human being whom no girl would ever touch in his short, morbidly unhappy life. The fact that Janis could assert otherwise was more evidence that the girl was unhinged. That she was also apparently into bestiality only confirmed it; the sicker it was, the more she wanted it. It was gross.

At school, Rufus's preoccupation with his own demise reached the point where he could no longer focus on a thing that was said in class and he did the previously unthinkable: he wagged school. When he went home he found Janis sitting in the kitchen, a giant bowl of ice-cream and a copy of the *Hamlin Encyclopaedia of Dermatology* open on the bench in front of her. She was supposed to be at school too, and they were both so preoccupied by their own sins (hers compounded by the ice-cream and gross book situation) that for a moment they each failed to register the other's guilt.

'I'm just ... !' they cried together. Then the penny dropped and they both fell into attitudes of sheepish complicity.

'This is really disgusting,' said Janis, gesturing at the book and resuming the spooning of ice-cream mouthwards. 'And yet somehow compelling.'

Rufus got a bowl and scooped himself a serve of the sickly, half-melted goop.

'Oh, my God! Look at that!' exclaimed Janis.

'I'd rather not.'

'What are you doing at home?' she asked, still studying the pages and sucking on her spoon.

'What are you doing? Mum won't be happy if she finds out.'

'Is she going to?' Janis arched her eyebrows at him meaningfully.

'That depends, I guess.' He arched his eyebrows back.

She stuck her spoon back into the container and scooped out another spoonful.

'Weren't you just sucking that?' said Rufus.

She put the spoon in her mouth and then slowly extracted it again, shiny and spotless, from her lips. She held it up: 'All clean, see?'

Rufus pushed away his bowl.

'So,' Janis closed the book, 'it's just you and me, huh? What are we going to do?'

Rufus felt the blood climbing into his face. That was another thing about him: he was a human embarrassment thermometer; he blushed like a period-drama virgin. 'What are we ... ?'

'... going to do? Do you think.' She propped her froggy face on her hands and blinked.

'I've got ... to study biology.'

'I could help with that.'

'No! No you couldn't.' Rufus started to get up.

'Why would you wag school in order to study?'

Rufus had to concede there was logic to that argument.

'Come on, Rufus. Why don't you watch telly with me? I won't bite.'

So they sat together on the sofa in the lounge room and watched *The Young and the Something*. Or *The Bold and the Something*. Anyhow the something and the something—Rufus wasn't really paying attention; he was too preoccupied with defending the coastline of his personal space. He'd be concentrating his efforts on repelling the invasion of a foot, and just when he thought he'd seen off that threat, a hand would sneak around the back of the sofa and start playing with his hair. If he tried to get up, she'd yank him back down again. He resolved to play dead. According to accepted theory, unwanted attentions will cease if you stop reacting to them. It had never worked before, but there was no reason to think it mightn't start to now. He gave up the fight and allowed Janis to lean against him, let her fingers twine in his curly nape, tolerated a hand that crept onto his knee, a mouth breathing hotly on his neck, a hand ...

Uh, oh! This was not going to work! He sprang up, rather uncomfortably. Once again she tried to drag him back down, but he shook her off.

Janis looked crestfallen. 'Aww, Rufie ...'

'Don't call me that. It's a date rape drug.'

After that, life got harder for Rufus. The awful fact was, Janis had turned him on, and unwelcome thoughts of her freckled hand sliding up his thigh now sullied the purity of his Fiona fantasies. Janis was everything a Fiona wasn't: she was ordinary-looking, she was vulgar, she was available, she was around. Christ, was she around! He was a fugitive in his own home.

In the meantime his cancer was progressing rapidly; he'd made the mistake of lifting his shirt slightly to scratch an itch and caught sight of a dark blemish about the size of a five-cent piece. A suffocating panic engulfed him. For fear of again catching sight of one of his tumours, Rufus took to showering at midnight with the light off and eyes squeezed painfully shut, just to make doubly sure they didn't open by accident. He developed a new appreciation for the challenges of the blind. Even when he mixed up the hot and cold taps and the water began to scald him, he kept his eyes resolutely closed, adjusting the taps by touch even as the temperature climbed towards the excruciating.

One night after his midnight shower, he got out to find that there was no towel on the rack. A naked, shut-eyed dash to his room was unthinkable, and it was too late to call out to anyone, so he had no choice but to drip dry. He was standing there naked, shivering in the dark, when he heard the door handle turn. In spite of himself, his eyes opened. He could have said something at that point, but in panic and embarrassment he hid behind the door instead. It was Janis, in her nightie, tip-toeing to the toilet, where she leaned over the bowl and began to hunt for her desensitised gag reflex with an index finger. He must have flinched because Janis caught a movement in the mirror, yelped and spun around.

There was Rufus, a skinny, wet tangle of limbs as he futilely tried to cover one bit of nakedness with another. 'Don't look! It's only me!'

Janis clutched at her chest. 'Oh, my fucking God, Rufus! You scared the living shit out of me!' Then she did a double-take. 'Are you naked?'

'Don't look! Please. Don't turn on the light!'

She began to snicker. 'What were you up to in here?'

'Nothing! I was just having a shower and I left my towel ... Please don't look!'

'Jesus, I'm not looking, okay? Not like I haven't seen it all before.'

There was an awkward silence. 'Can I have my clothes, please?' said Rufus at last.

'I can't find them.'

'Janis, please, not now. This is not funny. They're right next to you.'

'Sorry, can't find them.'

'I'll tell Mum you were throwing up again.'

'Don't you dare!' she hissed. 'I wasn't! And why are your eyes closed like that? What the hell's going on here?'

'I told you not to look!'

'Jesus, Rufus! I mean I know you're screwed up about sex and everything, but is it really such a big deal if I see your—'

But Rufus had started to cry. The dam of his defences, a psychological engineering project of years, was suddenly crumbling, all the anxiety and misery he'd been keeping pent up for so long crashing through the breach. He was coming apart, disintegrating into a snotty, foetal mess on the bathroom floor.

'Oh, baby!' said Janis, evincing maternal instincts she'd obviously scooped direct from the gene pool no thanks to nurture. She crouched down next to him where he was slumped on the tiles, his long pale back blue in the semi-darkness, and put a hand on the trembling, shuddering ridge of his spine. She stroked and muttered to him the meaningless, consoling syllables of motherly comfort—there there, now now—bewildered but moved nonetheless, tears of empathy starting in her own eyes. She knew what it meant to be turned inside out like this, to have her guts wrenched open.

He was saying something that she couldn't make out and she had to lean down close to hear the words through his sobs.

'How bad does it look?' he was saying.

'Baby, I don't know what you mean. I mean, you could work on those pecs, but ...'

'I'm dying, Janis.' He finally sat up enough that she could see his eyes, the whites of them pale in the darkened room.

'What are you talking about?'

'I have cancer.'

'Oh, my God! Rufus! Why didn't anyone tell me?'

'Nobody knows. I found this spot on my back and I recognised it as a melanoma from my dad's book, and a little after that I found these lumps in my neck. It's spread already. Look,' he said, gesturing at his bare chest.

Janis couldn't see much in the dark, so she went and turned on the light, ignoring Rufus's pleas. The glare seemed brutally stark and Rufus hid in his hands, whimpering and exposed as a shelled snail. She came and knelt on the floor beside him, gently inspected his chest and back.

'I still can't see anything.'

'What do you mean?'

'I can't see anything bad.'

Rufus allowed himself a glimpse through his fingers. To his amazement, his torso was white and unblemished as freshly fallen snow, apart from a familiar sprinkle of freckles in a pattern remarkably similar to the constellation of Virgo, and the red circle he'd recently glimpsed under his shirt, like a strawberry birthmark above his right hip. 'Look!' he said. 'There!'

Janis ran her fingertip over it. It was rough and raised, slightly peeling. 'Well I'm no doctor, but that doesn't look ... eczema maybe?'

'What about this then?' said Rufus, standing up and turning around to show her.

'What?'

'Can't you see, in the middle of my back? It's a melanoma! Look at the dark centre and the paler, asymmetrical outer part. It's textbook!'

'It just looks like a mole to me. But maybe you should get it checked out if you're so worried about it.'

'But the lumps in my neck! Here ...' He turned around and took Janis's hand, guiding her fingers to the place beneath his jaw, into the sinews where the blood pulsed and beat along its secret courses, into the slender muscle that curved down his neck. There was tenderness and concern in her fingers, the way they listened to his heartbeat. He swallowed, his Adam's apple bobbing against her fingertips.

'Lymph glands,' she said, and very gently took hold of his penis.

'Oh, no,' said Rufus.

'I'd have thought that was good news,' said Janis.

'I meant—'

'So did I,' she whispered, and kissed him.

Rufus didn't know how to kiss, though he supposed it couldn't hurt to try something like this. And when somehow or other his hands found their way under Janis's nightie, he hadn't the faintest idea what to do with all the warm, buoyant flesh he found there: her quivering bottom, her loose pointy breasts. Though she didn't seem to mind when his hands found something to do nonetheless. The light went off, and the nightie puddled on the floor, and Janis lay on the nightie, and Rufus floundered on her hot, sighing body like a fish, his knees slapping on the tiles, his back silvered by the light of moon or streetlight. And because it was increasingly apparent that his Fiona fantasies had got it all terribly wrong, and because he was probably completely mistaken about the cancer too... well Rufus just lost all his confidence, and had to make it up as he went along.

It was only later, as he lay in his bed, floating in a night filled with blue like the bottom of the sea, that Rufus thought of Janis's fingers touching his pulse and discovered that a strange new sickness had supplanted the one he'd just lost. What it might mean Rufus couldn't say, but he could feel it swelling in the space beneath his breastbone. An aching, a beating, a fluttering, like too many butterflies trying to get out.

Croc

Kelly came out of the 7-Eleven with her ciggies and her chuppa-chups and the white Commodore was there again. It had been there earlier, slowing down to match her pace as she walked along the footpath. She'd looked up and seen the driver's silhouetted head turned to her through the tinted windows, the shape of an afro wig like Krusty the Clown. Fear squirted into her blood. She told herself not to run. To run would turn this into a chase. She looked straight ahead and the car idled along beside her. He was in no hurry. Ahead was the main road, cars swishing past in the grey afternoon. Maybe if she reached it she'd be safe—but she knew that wasn't true. Anything could happen anywhere. Then the car revved hard and took off, making her jump with fright before the relief flooded in and she had to sit down on the low brick fence of someone's garden because her legs were shaking so hard.

But now there he was again, or a car that looked just the same; she couldn't see the driver through the windscreen glare. She dodged along the side of the 7-Eleven. There was a narrow lane that ran down the back and if Krusty wanted to follow her, he'd have his work cut out in that big car. The thing was trying to work out what it meant. Was it a warning from Croc, a way of telling her he had eyes everywhere, he had people? Or was it worse? Had she done something wrong and he intended to teach her a lesson? Or was it nothing to do with Croc at all? Was it just some dickhead trying to freak her out, was she going crazy?

Around the corner two kids sat against the wall behind the skip, thin legs stretched out, chroming. She started a little, had to step over them. One of them called out to her: *Hey, dude, wassup?* She ignored him, ducked under the railing, down into the lane. She heard the other kid: *Stuck-up bitch.* But she was already running.

On Saturdays Kelly worked at Pets 4 U. She'd always wanted to be a vet when she was growing up; there was nothing she loved more than animals. Of course she didn't know then how smart you had to be— smarter than a normal doctor even. She'd cried and cried when she heard that. So then she'd thought about being a vet nurse. Maybe she could still do that one day. She'd go back and finish high school and then... well, she wasn't sure how you became a vet nurse, but she supposed there was a course or something. She'd have these thoughts, and then she'd remember her situation. Of course she couldn't go back to school. But Croc did at least let her keep her job at the pet shop, and even if it was mainly putting stock on the shelves and serving customers, she didn't mind because she was close to animals the whole day. Just walking in, hearing the clamour of the budgies, catching that strong animal whiff, made her feel good. Sometimes she got to feed them, and Mr Nguyen didn't mind if she picked up the puppies and stroked them, because dogs need love as well as food and water.

Mr Nguyen was an alright boss. When Kelly ran away from home, she'd stopped showing up for work at the shop. She was living on people's sofas, in youth refuges, sometimes sleeping rough, and she'd lose track of which day it was, or she'd be in some suburb miles away, and then weeks had gone by and she felt too embarrassed to go back. But later, when Rhona, her youth worker, had found her some transitional accommodation, she started thinking about the shop again, got to feeling like it was the one thing in her life that she'd looked forward to, that she was actually good at. It wasn't just that she liked the animals; they liked her too. She had a way with them, everybody said so. So one Saturday morning she put on her blue Pets 4 U work shirt and caught the eight o'clock bus to the plaza. There was a new girl there of course—why hadn't she thought of that?—and she had half-turned to walk out again when Mr Nguyen appeared from the back room.

Kelly!

Hello Mr Nguyen, she said, heat rising into her face.

He took in her shirt, her neat hair.

Your mother she come looking for you. Many time.

I'm sorry Mr Nguyen.

A good daughter not make her mother to worry so much.

She hung her head.

He studied her. Your mother I think she very ... he searched for the word ... She no make easy for Australian girl like you, always want free. Different Vietnamese girl.

Kelly looked at the floor.

But she mother still.

Yes Mr Nguyen.

It was dim in the aisles of the shop, a grey glare hard in the front window. A girl, maybe five, dragging her harried mother over to peer at the fumbling litter of golden retrievers in the shopfront. Mr Nguyen's face looked tired and old in the pallid light, as if he had been as worried lately as Kelly's mother. She wondered about his kids—he had a daughter not much younger than Kelly—and for some reason the thought made her chest ache.

Laura! he called out.

The new girl, who'd been busy tidying a display, keeping out of the way, came out from behind the counter.

Yes, Mr Nguyen?

This is Kelly. She starting today. You her boss. Congratulation.

The girl, so young-looking she might still be in high school, looked incredulous. She turned to Kelly with an embarrassed smile, muttered a hi.

Kelly offered to clean out the budgie cage. With the bucket of soapy water in her hand, she felt so happy she almost cried.

Kelly met Croc at his fortieth birthday. A Goth girl at the youth refuge she was staying at knew someone, invited her along. The place was full of Bandidos, their Harleys lining the street, their shiny leather-clad backs clustered like beetles around the barbie. Megadeth blasting, the stink of burning meat, and a bathtub full of ice and VB on the lawn. She sat on the couch in the front room and someone passed her a line tapped out on the back of a magazine. Leaning back in the sofa, the bitter trickle of speed in the back of her throat, she noticed the crocodile paraphernalia for the first time. Posters and photos, a set of teeth on the shelf, a stuffed head grinning from the wall.

Later, she sat with the blokes in the yard drinking beer and smoking points of meth out of a broken lightbulb. She felt good, clear and strong despite the boozy spin in her head. Running away had been right, she saw. She was grown up, she was wild. For the first time in so long, under this black sky with these bad men, freedom and danger in her blood, she felt there were possibilities for her. Bikers, she kept thinking. Her parents would flip.

She drank some more and smoked some weed and the garden spun. The Goth girl was making out with one of the guys, his hand round her shoulder going down inside her top and grabbing her tit, but the girl didn't mind. The pins in her tongue moved between his lips. And one of the bikers went and pissed on the leg of some kid who shouldn't have been there in the first place, who was he kidding? The biker just flopped it out and stood there pissing and laughing, the kid not noticing at first, then he felt the warmth and he didn't know what to do, so he just let the guy piss on him, steam coming off his jeans and piss running down into his sneakers. Later, someone had a .22. He slurred, staggered, fired at the sky like he wanted to murder the stars, and Kelly rolled over and threw up into the thistles.

She went inside to get a glass of water to clear the sour taste from her mouth and someone blocked her with an arm across the hallway. Croc. She'd seen him turning steaks on the barbecue, a fanged laugh, air of control. They respected him, she saw that. He'd seen her too, eyes locking a moment before Kelly looked away. He had noticed her.

He was thin and wiry, with long lines and creases in his swarthy face that made him look older than forty, greying sideburns. Not handsome exactly, but she sensed his power, a cold electricity when his yellow eyes slid over her body.

He rested his cigarette hand on the wall next to her. So tell me ...

Tell you what? Her skin prickled at his closeness, his unbuttoned shirt, his animal smell of sweat mixed with booze and cigarettes.

He tucked back a stray strand of her hair, grinning in a way that made her shiver. Fear, excitement: she couldn't tell. Whatever you want, he said.

He was far too old for her, but his interest flattered her. She'd seen the way the bikies acted around him, laughing at his jokes, deferring. Afraid even. Her face burned in the heat of his gaze, his hungry, sexual smile. Normally she'd have been too shy to open up, but the meth was at work, she was holed up in the corner, and the only release from the pressure was to talk. So she started to tell him about herself, and in the end told him more than she'd meant to. Even about that last summer at home when it all got out of control and she'd picked up a kitchen knife in a fight with her dad and he'd thrown her to the ground and nearly broken her wrist. How he'd started to cry and the wheezing sound of it frightened her more than his violence. She'd wanted to break him, she realised, to find out at last what was inside that tight, angry exterior, but when it actually happened she'd freaked.

Croc laughed. Oh poor Dad. So we have a wild one, do we? And you look so sweet.

Fuck off—she said it to prove she was tough, unafraid, but even in her own ears it sounded childish—I hate that word.

He raised an eyebrow, amused. Ah, so you're a bad girl, are you?

He went to toke on his cigarette and the ash broke and fell down her front. He made a fuss of brushing it off, his hands lingering as they swept her breasts.

It was when she mentioned the pet shop though, how much she loved animals, that a glint came into Croc's eyes.

I think I have something you might like to see.

Really?

But only if you don't tell anyone. You can keep a secret, can't you, Kelly?

Cross my heart.

He took her out into the backyard and unlocked a large shed, glancing around to make sure no-one else was looking, then flicked on the light and closed the door behind them. In the centre of the room was a huge aquarium tank, maybe two and a half metres long and half as wide. The crocodile inside it must have grown in the time he'd had it, because it could no longer fit at full stretch. Its nose and tail touched the glass at either end. It lay on a bed of sand, half submerged in filthy green water. Its eyes were tiny ponds of evil.

Oh. My. God. She looked at Croc. You can't be serious …

She walked around it, awestruck, even dared to stand a foot away from where its nose rested against the glass. A single tooth curled from its pale lip. It showed no sign of recognising her presence, but the alien sentience in its unblinking eyes prickled on her skin. Gobbets of fur and gore stained the sand near its head.

Are you allowed to keep that?

He gave a barking laugh.

How'd you get it then?

Contacts. Money. He shrugged, took a drag. They can get you pretty much anything.

The crocodile moved, and Kelly jumped.

You're not scared of him, are ya, Kelly?

No.

Really?

He flicked the light switch and darkness snapped shut on her. She screamed. The blackness swam and her hand, shooting out for something solid, touched glass. She yanked it back again, her hairs standing up at the thought of the thing there in the dark beside her.

Then a light. Croc had turned on a torch, was holding it under his chin so it made hideous, vampiric shadows, laughing fit to bust. *Boo.*

Fuck off, that wasn't funny.

She ducked for the door, escaped back onto the lawn, the cold air of the amphetamine-sharpened night.

Stay, he told her, as long as you like. I don't mind. Kelly had nowhere to go but back to the youth refuge, where some jerk kept trying to feel her arse whenever the duty worker turned his back, so she decided she would stay—just for a bit. She was still at Croc's when the yard paled with dawn, still there when the last Harley was gone from the street and the stench of puke and spilled beer in the backyard began to thicken in the rising heat. She was still there when, in the afternoon, the meth at last gave way and a tidal wave of exhaustion swamped her. Did Croc give her a pill to help kill the last agitation of her limbs? She couldn't remember. But she did remember a dream of lying on Croc's bed, crushed beneath an ocean of fatigue, while someone removed her clothes. She did remember her leaden limbs and the suffocating heat of the room and a numb claustrophobia as she tried to lift her head. She remembered being dragged down a river by her feet, going under, coming up, the sun hot and bright as a burn on her face and the crocodile on top of her, a hurt inside her while she tried to keep her head above water, to stop herself from drowning. Then the surface closing over her again, down into a darkness the colour of the blood of her eyelids, a dream without a story or faces or places, just a space that got smaller and smaller and smaller without ever completely vanishing.

She woke at last from a sleep so deep she had no sense of its duration. The dull light might have been evening or early morning. She was lying clothed on Croc's bed. The room was empty, the house quiet. Her skull thumped. She got up and went into the living room. It was tidy as if the party had never been. She went to the backyard. Croc was laid back in a chair, drinking a beer. She saw from the sky it was evening.

She lives!

He grinned, tipped back the stubby. She hesitated. Did you ... did we ...?

What?

She couldn't read his expression. She bit her lip, uncertain of herself now.

Have a sausage, he said. They're good.

There was a boy once, at school. Josh Desosa. An olive-skinned boy with a face as pretty as a girl's, the wrong kind of beautiful for a place like that. They put so much shit on him, trying to ruin him, but whatever it did to him inside never touched his face. Nothing could mar the perfection of his mouth or his eyes. He was a quiet kid, not many friends. But for some reason he had a big crush on Kelly. In class she'd glance up to catch his look, those almost black eyes, quickly averted. Lining up in the corridor he'd deliberately stand close and for a few seconds as he lingered next to her, there'd be this moment, a liquid electricity on her skin that made her flush. She didn't like that. Then he asked her out. That really surprised her, that he had it in him. To some dumb Jackie Chan movie at the local multiplex. During the film he took her hand. It was so sweet and old-fashioned, and she should have liked it but instead it made her feel messed up.

After the film she took him round into the shopping centre loading bay and pressed him up against the concrete wall and kissed him, put her hand in his pants and jerked his cock till he gave a sob and came stickily on her arm. She knew she'd ruined it. She wiped her arm off on the wall and tried to offer him a cigarette, but he couldn't even look at her. She thought he was going to cry and she didn't want to see it so she told him she had to be somewhere and went home, ablaze with confusion and anger and guilt, not understanding herself at all, why she was such a bad person.

She thought of it sometimes still: the sensation of Josh's hand steady in the dark of the cinema. That intolerable tenderness that she knew she could find no place for. She wished she was someone else: a better, kinder person. Croc was what she deserved. It was curious how her heart had raced with threat at the softness of that boy's hand while it beat only dully faster when Croc frightened her.

Croc was not tender. At the start he could be charming, magnetic, attentive—but never tender. Early on there had been something she had wanted from him, apart from the drugs. She'd longed for him to look at her again with the rapt attention of that first night, his gaze telling her she meant something, was somebody. And in the beginning he had showered her with gifts, which she'd been happy for, even if they were really presents for someone older than her. But his smile had gone cold so fast. She was helpless against this erosion of contempt, hated herself for not knowing how to stop it. Then his cruelty emerged.

One day Croc coming home smiling: I have something for you.

Another present?

Only a week before he'd done the same thing and given her perfume, which she'd worn to please him.

You deserve it. Come here. She came. Now put out your hand and close your eyes.

She stood there smiling and he ground his cigarette out in her open palm. She jerked back from the pain and then she was on the floor, the side of her face ringing with the force of his slap. He knelt in front of her.

You went out today, didn't you?

He was so calm. He put the tip of his boot on her fingertips. Leaned.

What did I say about going out? Only when and where I say.

Stop it, she sobbed. Why are you doing this?

Because you're a little fucking liar. The last two words through gritted teeth, his foot grinding on her fingers.

She could never predict him. There was nothing to read in his face to let you know what he'd do next. She became attuned to the slightest nuances of his deadpan face—found secret tells in his neck muscles, read her own body for shivers of danger.

But then there were certain rituals that always followed the same pattern, when she knew exactly what was coming. Like his TV days, when he'd spend a whole day watching Foxtel Sports and drinking beer, from ten in the morning till after midnight. He'd stare for hours at cars going round a track, the waspish whine of the engines and the muffled hype of the commentator coming dull through the wall to where Kelly sat in the dark of the bedroom, picking at scabs on her knees or pulling balls of fluff off her jumper or chewing her fingernails down till they bled. Then eventually he'd call her in and make her sit watching too—sport, always sport. The endless, frustrated run-and-crunch, run-and-crunch of NRL, or the same reeling blue sky with the same golf ball in it. A crowd of riders snaking down a mountain road, their bikes all leaning as one like a flock of flat, mechanical birds. The light flickering blue on Croc's lifeless face as he watched, the cigarette smog thickening, the ashtray overflowing, the stack of empties growing beside his chair.

But this game wasn't about the sport on TV. It was about his sport. Around six or seven he'd switch to porn, his eyes following every scene with the same expressionless stare, but a new level of tension in the air. He was indifferent to the porn, but it turned him on in a different way to play with her, knowing how she hated it. She'd learned to sit still, as still as she could on the speed he'd given her earlier, probably because he knew this was coming. Then he'd say disgusting things to get a reaction, and she'd deaden herself against it, and against the things on the screen, learnt a sort of strict mental discipline, a very controlled kind of spacing out, in order to cope with the tremendous urge to scream. He drew it out, hours sometimes, until the time came when he made her come over and do what it was he wanted her to do.

She waited for Saturdays, when she could work at the pet shop. Even serving the customers felt good, just talking to people. And she'd formed a sort of friendship with Laura over time. Laura was two years older than her, but Kelly always thought of her as the younger one. It was always Kelly telling Laura how to do stuff, how to make sure the acidity level was right in the fish tank, or getting her out of muddles with the cash register. Laura left school in Year Ten because she didn't like school work, and 'because'. She married her boyfriend at eighteen, only a year before she started at the shop, and one day came in bursting with the news she was pregnant, a fate that Kelly dreaded more than anything. She was so straight Kelly could never tell her about her life. But they mucked around together and Laura's talk about stuff on TV or her plans for the baby room gave Kelly a good feeling.

One afternoon when it was really quiet and Mr Nguyen was out, the silliest mood came over the two girls. Kelly started taking out the puppies one by one and putting them on the floor of the shop, and they all headed off in different directions, snuffling the ground and excited. Laura was laughing even while she begged Kelly to stop and put them back, worried that Mr Nguyen would come back and they'd both get in trouble. She rushed around trying to catch the puppies faster than Kelly could get them back out again, and there were puppies scrabbling for the doors and the two girls in hysterics, their sides aching, and Laura struggling to get control of herself because she really was freaked at the idea of getting in trouble—I'm serious! she shrieked—but the harder she tried, the more she doubled up.

Afterwards, though, when she went home, Kelly always remembered to put on a bad mood. She too kept her disguises.

She remembered the night she ran away, the moment it became clear that she could do this, that she was serious, and they couldn't stop her. Nobody could stop her. It was as if a sort of film broke and all of a sudden she could see the world clearly. Running her hand along a wet metal rail, sweeping the water under her palm, she felt naked to the touch of things, like she could really feel for the first time. It was cold, she walked along the Nepean Highway and the lights of the cars shone off the wet, the tyres hissed and made tracks through the neon and she walked and walked, and slept under a bridge, woke up to her beating heart and stared up at the dull stars and thought, *Who am I?* She felt swollen with her lostness and her anger and her bravery. She would survive—like this, like a wild animal if she had to.

But now here she was, on her knees in the bathtub, scrubbing Ajax into the gleaming enamel for the fourth time today because she had to do something with the restlessness. The house stank of bleach and everything was scoured back and spotless and she was so lonely she almost wished Croc would come home just for someone to talk to. He'd said to her, no TV. How would he know if she did watch? But she was scared he had some way, a hidden camera somewhere or something. She'd found cameras before. Scrub, scrub. Or he'd come home and catch her before she had a chance to flick the remote.

Her hands were a mess. She bit a loose point of skin beside her nail, stripped it back with her teeth and winced at the pain. A bobby-pin of blood welled. She'd have liked to sit on the couch again and watch *Home and Away* with her sister and argue about who was hotter, Aden or Ric. Christ, she'd even have liked to see her mum and dad right now. She tore another corner of skin down, nibbled at the root. Fuck it, don't cry. Don't fucking cry. Scrub, scrub. But it came, she couldn't stop it. Shoulders shaking in the bathtub, she watched her tears run down the sparkling enamel.

She stood in the living room, no energy now, just a shell. Gazing at the street through the cheap lacy curtains that let her look out, but hid her from view. Number fifteen across the way: What goes on in there? she wondered. What secrets does it hide? Do you see me, number fifteen? Do you see that shadow through the curtains?

If only she could sleep. Day, night meant nothing. She'd lost the sense of them, slept sometimes randomly during the day, spent the night wide awake. A permanent jet lag when she wasn't speeding. Outside it was windy, the prunus trees on the nature strip agitated. The whole world was scoured down, abraded back to its bones. And her mind was the same, empty like that street, but endlessly moved by a wind that tossed and spun and blew nowhere.

Then she saw the car, a white Commodore parked across the street and down a ways. Inside, the shadow of a head, not moving. She stepped back from the window. It probably wasn't the same person, she told herself. And people sit in cars, don't they? Maybe he was visiting someone at a certain time and he'd arrived early. Or maybe he liked the song on the radio and didn't want to get out until it was finished. But half an hour later she checked and he was still there. And two hours later, even as it began to darken, there was still that unmoving head. Her bones felt so cold, she wanted to take a bath in that too-clean tub, but she was afraid to be naked.

She mustn't lose her mind. She went to visit Ange the other day to get her meth, and wondered if Ange was losing it. She looked bad, with nasty sores on her face and hands, white and skinny as hell. Sorry love, she said, her hand hovering near the bloody crater on her cheek, I been pickin' again. Ange had an ex who used to hit her, did stuff to her much worse than Croc had ever done to Kelly. Croc had bruised her forehead pretty badly one day when he threw an ashtray at her, he'd burnt and hit her, but he never broke a bone or put her in the hospital or anything like what Brian had done to Ange. She got away from him, but she reckoned he'd found her again, that he was hiding around the house at night. The worst thing was he'd got into the roof. She'd heard him up there moving around at night. So Ange had gone up herself and scattered broken glass everywhere. She'd got the bastard too. See? she said, holding up a sliver of glass stained rusty with blood. Her mouth twitched into a smile, fell back to a quivering line.

Fucker. We might not be able to get away from 'em, but we can mess with 'em too, right?

Rhona, Kelly's youth worker, once said you got like that on meth: hearing things in the walls, worms under your skin, shit like that, but then Rhona hadn't seen the blood on the glass.

They did some ice and then went outside into the sunny front garden. On the nature strip next door there was a whole lot of junk waiting for the hard garbage, including an old photocopier, and suddenly they both had the idea they'd like to take it apart and see how it worked, so that's what they did for the next hour or so, pulling apart that photocopier and every little bit inside it until they'd reduced it to a pile of scrap. And still they had that meth-driven urge to do, so they pulled apart a TV and a computer as well. It was funny. They had a good time, sitting on the nature strip in the sun and laughing as they picked metal and plastic apart with their fingers.

When Croc was gone he left bags of meat for her to feed the crocodile. Early on she dreamt of poisoning it with Ratsak. But now she knew she could never do it. It wasn't the crocodile's fault that it had the misfortune of being loved by a bad man. More than anything she felt pity for the beast. It was grotesquely large for the tank now, its spine bent and contorted, sores on its head where it chafed the glass every day. One of its eyes had a fungal infection of some kind. She could see it was dying for the things natural to it: reeds and mud and the slide into dark water.

She sat there in the dimness of the shed and it watched her, waiting for her to throw in the next bit of meat. When she did, sometimes it fell in a place where the crocodile couldn't reach it, and it would go berserk, twisting and thrashing about before finally falling still again. She did her best to fish those pieces out with a net on a pole that she also used to try to clean up its shit, but there were always some pieces left to rot. The tank was fast becoming a sewer, but she was too scared of the crocodile to bucket out the water and refill it, even though it could never turn around far enough to bite her. On hot days she had to hold her nose against the reek.

One Saturday when they'd finished work, Laura and Kelly came out of the pet-shop and Croc was parked outside. He grinned at them from behind sunglasses, winding down the window.

Is that your dad? said Laura.

No, he's, he's ... just a friend—she was so flustered it came out flat, false. She saw the confusion on Laura's face.

Hey, Croc called from the car. Who's your friend?

I better go, said Kelly.

You don't want to get a milkshake anymore? Why don't you bring your friend ...

No, no, really. I forgot I got stuff to do.

Hey, Croc called to Laura. Come here.

Laura went over, smiling, unsure of herself, and Croc talked to her while Kelly hung back, chewing her nails. She watched him leaning out the window, joking around with her, hairy forearm resting on the hot metal of the car door, two blinding suns in the black glass that hid his eyes.

After a while he let her go and she came back, smiled at Kelly uncertainly. He's nice, she said.

She left it a few days before she told Croc she was giving up the job.

Really, he said, wearing that all-purpose smile. And why's that?

She shrugged, studied her fingernails.

No reason?

Dunno. It's boring. She looked at him, challenging.

He went on smiling. Only his eyes narrowed a little. You're a pathetic loser, you know that?

Late summer and here's Kelly dialling a number with shaking hands. She wasn't supposed to use the phone—he'd taken her mobile too— but she didn't care. She couldn't bear being alone in the house a second longer.

Hello? came the voice.

Hello, Laura? It's Kelly.

Kelly! What happened to you? We were so worried. Mr Nguyen even called your parents. He still owes you pay I think.

Sorry, I ... She couldn't think of an excuse that made sense.

Are you okay?

Fine. She scratched the table with a fingernail. She was at a loss for what to say, she'd forgotten how to talk to people.

So I had the baby, Laura said at last. I'm a mother, can you believe it?

Cool! Is it, what did you … ?

It's a boy, Jesse. Nine and a half pounds. Well, he's bigger than that now of course. He's a real heifer, just like his dad. Say, why don't you come visit? I'm alone so much at home you know.

Kelly wanted to. When she'd called she'd meant to, and she took the address, said she'd come right over. But the hot street seemed to hum with menace, even though there was no-one in sight. She never stepped out the door.

Croc was gone and the house clicked and whirred. The refrigerator turned itself on and off, a tree scraped the wall. A disconnected percussion of tiny sounds. A cockroach scuttled in the kitchen and she could hear the hairs on its legs chafing the lino. A blowfly sozzled between the flywire and the kitchen window, black shells clustered on the sill. Silence as it stopped, walked the glass, then the buzzing started again. Over and over, the silence, then the buzzing. She waited by the window for the fly to land, slammed her hand against the mesh. Maggots writhed on the pane.

She lay in bed, the curtains closed. The house whispered, words just under the threshold of sense. She covered her ears with the pillow.

In the night she woke with a sudden, cold certainty. All the pieces fell together and it was all horribly clear. She got up, found a screwdriver and turned the phone upside down on the floor of the hall. She had to be very careful to put it all back together right so he wouldn't notice it. It was hard, her hands shaking so much she kept spilling the tiny screws. Yes, there it was, she knew it. He'd put something inside the receiver. So he knew she'd called Laura. He'd heard Laura give Kelly her address, knew how she was so often home alone. A dry spasm of nausea made her stomach tighten.

She knew she shouldn't call anyone again. But she had to know. She could just call and hang up when Laura answered. Then at least she'd know she was safe. She picked up the receiver and dialled.

Come on.

She counted the rings. Five, six, then click, Laura's cheerful voice. Hi, you've reached John, Laura and Jesse's place, please leave a message.

The Commodore. Was the Commodore there? She got down on her hands and knees and crawled into the front room, made her way towards the curtains. Her neck prickled. She turned and looked up and the stuffed crocodile head on the wall was swelling and shrinking and leering at her. She crawled over to the wall and turned on the light to make it stop. But now all the windows were black and looking in at her cowering against the wall in her nightie, shivering despite the stifling heat. She flicked the switch back off again and went back into the hall.

It was the middle of the night—of course she'd got the answering machine. But if she called again, they'd pick up, surely. They'd worry it was bad news. She dialled again. Come on, Laura, please answer. Answer the phone. Answer the phone.

Ring ring ... ring ring ... ring ring. Then the message again.

Again and again she called. Always the click, the cheery message. Now she was going to be sick. She made it to the toilet, threw up the pizza she'd had for dinner. Somewhere she had some speed. In the kitchen. She was shaking and the contents of the drawer fell on the floor. Shit. She stuffed the things back in the drawer, but couldn't get it back on its tracks properly, it went in all wrong. She found a gram of head in a plastic sleeve, but no speed. The other room. There it was. Thank God, thank Jesus. She wanted to smoke it, but that would take too long. She needed it right away, sniffed it straight out of the foil.

Morning and Kelly was in the kitchen cutting gashes in a chicken and stuffing them with Valium. She took it out to the shed and threw it to the crocodile, which snapped it up in one. An hour later she let herself back into the shed. She was disappointed to find it still awake. But when she came closer she saw she was wrong. It was fast asleep with its eyes open. She waved a lump of meat over it and it didn't stir. She took a crowbar from the wall and heaved it into the glass. It caved, fell in a thousand shards. Sand and water poured out onto the floor, spilling with them an overpowering stink of ammonia and rotted meat. She walked around the tank, smashing every pane. The sand poured out, and the crocodile slid with it onto the concrete. Free of the tank, she saw how truly huge it was. She bent to touch it for the first time as it lay in the sand and broken glass. She stroked its snout. Such dry, alien skin, like touching something dead, artificial. The animal's infected eye was almost closed over, possibly blind, and there were other patches of infection, a veil of something white and scabrous extending over its skin.

She knelt low and lifted its lip, saw the feared teeth. Then she stood, brushing the sand from her jeans, got a broom and swept up the glass. She left the shed door open.

Kelly stood in the kitchen. A cloudless day, lawnmower song rising and falling. She looked out into the backyard and saw the crocodile, huge and still on the lawn, a monstrous ornament. Next door, the neighbour was pruning his peach tree. Snip, snip. The branches fell.

She went outside onto the sunny front lawn. She looked left and right. There was the white Commodore. She'd worked it out now. She was sure she knew. She walked straight at it.

She could see his clown's hair. She banged on the dark glass with her fist.

Let down the window!

The man inside stared straight ahead.

Let down the window. I want to talk to you.

His face was impassive.

You're a cop, aren't you? Come on, you can tell me.

He turned the ignition key.

Come on. Tell me why you're watching him. What's he done?

The car started to slide forward. She ran with it, still hammering on the glass.

Who is he? What's he done? I want to know! Please.

The car moved away, faster now. She ran after it, banging on the boot until she couldn't keep up anymore, was left on the road. She watched it reach the stop sign, indicating left. She sat down on the kerb and put her head in her hands, her face between her knees. Her face was itching so badly. It was the worms she'd caught from Croc. She was going to need something to get them out.

Tornado

After I'd thrown in my medical degree, signing three forms in front of a disapproving woman in student admin; after I'd told my parents I needed time to 'find myself' and my mother had turned her back on me; after I'd sold off the small package of shares they'd given me for my twenty-first, and driven out of Adelaide on a Tuesday morning in late summer when the city was at work, I found myself in the backyard of a house in St Kilda so close to Luna Park I could hear the clatter-rush of the train going down the first drop of the Scenic Railway, trailing screams into the balmy late afternoon air. The two girls sat on dilapidated white wooden chairs, drinking Coronas with lemon wedged in the glass throats. Oh, they found everything faintly amusing—tittering and twinkling and cool as the bottles that dangled loose in their fingers. I sat there and the conversation drifted cryptically between the two of them, passing me by. Occasionally they remembered to ask me some question, their attention wandering the moment I started to speak. Mary and Jane, so urbane. Though it was Jane who mesmerised me, the image of some twenties poster girl with her dark bob and her doll's face, and something serious in her eyes when they caught mine, even while her lips remained tweaked with irony. Midges eddied over the grass, and the screams from the Scenic Railway drifted across; and then, after seeming to barely register my existence, they told me the room was mine if I wanted it and when did I want to move in?

So later that evening, I chucked an Adidas bag full of clothes into the corner of a musty room at the front of the house. I closed the door and flung myself down on the mattress in the corner to soak in the house's heavy quiet while images of the past days flashed against the black of my eyelids: the long, tedious road, the glittering blue bite of Port Phillip Bay. Flickering faces, the white shimmering heat rising off Acland Street. Then the shift to stranger landscapes, dreams, sleep.

Mary and Jane had been friends since primary school. Sometimes they jumped into bed together in the mornings like sisters on Easter Sunday, to giggle hysterically about Secret Girls' Business. They tickled one another, romped about in their pyjamas, and I would creep past their door, tip-toeing, either because I didn't want them to stop or because I was afraid of their laughter turning on me—its lightness always seemed to edge on mockery. And then there was the thrill, sharpened by the fear of being caught, of listening in the hallway outside Jane's room—thinking of her fleecy blue pyjamas and the warm bare breasts inside them as she rolled about giggling with Mary.

They both smoked weed almost daily, sometimes bongs at ten in the morning, in the living room with the sun coming through an inverted sea of cannabis fog. Or before they went out at night, after the whole girly ritual of fussing and primping and shoes, their last act to pull down a cone, tottering out the door with the smoke still locked in their lungs like a fortifier. But it was Mary who had the hard taste in drugs, popping pills for fun on Friday night, snorting coke and sometimes smack, speeding on Saturday and coming down with another bong on Sunday morning. And the little kitchen was always cluttered with bottles and smelt of Southern Comfort and stale beer.

It felt dangerous to me, and thrilling—*fuck you, Dad, look at me now.* For him there was no hard, no soft, there were just drugs. Just dopeheads and junkies and scumbags. I accepted the bong when it was passed around, though to start with I burped nauseating smoke and spiralled into a panic I didn't dare show, lying in the bean bag and having to wrest open my eyes to find some solid reference point, to stop myself tumbling into the void that yawned and reeled at the back of my mind. One time staggering to the toilet to barf into the bowl. Paranoia would seize me: Mary's friends sitting round and smirking about me, seeing what I really was: a straight-laced dork from Glenelg who'd only ever fucked one girl in his life and who until a month ago had been a friggin' med student who didn't know what an 'e' was. Who'd voted for Howard because that's what my arsehole dad did for Christ's sake.

Mary was an artist—or so she was happy to call herself when asked what she did. Her oeuvre, a series of women with prominent vulvas, was pinned to the walls of the house: blue vulva-woman, gold vulva-woman, green vulva-woman, and I tried to look impressed though I was secretly baffled. To my untutored eye, the execution seemed abysmal, like a Sixth-grader's attempt at Picasso's *Weeping Woman*, but I never pretended to understand much about art. To me it sometimes seemed the only thing about art was that it was on a gallery wall.

I had no idea what I wanted to do, and right then I didn't care. I was living off the money from the shares and the few bucks I could scrape together busking on my guitar. Nobody knew where I was. Neither my parents nor the few friends I'd kept from high school, relationships that had fallen into little more than drinking and the same empty jibes that seemed to hide a deeper ennui. I just told them I was going to Melbourne and left it at that. I was free to shed who I'd been, be whatever, whoever I wanted. I had plans, scribbled in a notebook that grew thinner and thinner as I tore out the pages.

I'd have been anyone for Jane, whatever it was she loved, if only I could have discerned the pattern. She seemed to reserve her love for the least likely and worthy objects: Datsuns, old matchboxes, pigeons. Anything conspicuously beautiful or popular left her cold. Some indecipherable form of cool, which came full circle, made Sinatra's cheesy crooning in again, though probably not if I'd listened to it. For a while she spoke of her crush on a certain guy selling CDs at the second-hand music shop on Barkly Street. Ooh, she'd gush to Mary, he's so cute! Screwing up her nose in that way she had. So I, sick with jealousy, went to the shop in question, standing there flicking through the racks in a desultory fashion while looking for the guy she meant. Expecting some über-handsome half-shaved dude, but the only candidate I could see was a stooping, older guy with round glasses, shabby clothes and unkempt hair already retreating from a bony, academic brow. When I finally decided this had to be the bloke she meant, I wasn't sure what to feel: better or worse. Feminine affection was a stranger thing than I'd given it credit for.

There were times I longed to say one honest thing to her. To tell her what it did to me when she came out of the bathroom after her morning shower in that red satin dressing-gown. For a moment with her wet sleek hair she was a geisha girl, an oriental concubine. She would lean forward to dry her hair over the blow heater, and in the open neck of her gown I'd catch sight of the tantalising valley between her soap-fragrant breasts. One time a whole bosom, round as a pear and milky pale, a glimpse of rosy nipple. She was as oblivious to me as if I'd been a cat there on the sofa. I wanted to say stop it. I wanted to say do it more. But I sat there with my cornflakes in my lap enacting a self-conscious nonchalance, trying to conceal my stolen glances among others cast at harmless objects: a book on a shelf, a candle, a picture on the wall. And then caught Mary's look from across the room. Her habitually amused mouth, but her eyes narrow and cat-like and glinting.

So, she said to me once in the kitchen, you like Jane, don't you?

That smile again, those same narrowed eyes.

I was caught on the hop. Of course, I said, stiffly. She's very nice. Turning away to busy myself with tidying a bench top.

I thought so.

I tried to protest: I just mean she's nice. I like her, you know. I mean, of course I do.

You don't have a chance you know.

That hit me in the guts. It's not like that, I said, weakly.

I mean: you. Look at her.

I turned around, stricken. She was still smiling, but her mouth twitched with a barely repressed passion. I couldn't understand it.

One day we piled into Mary's old Holden and drove out to a wet patch of bush near Trentham to hunt for magic mushrooms. It was just the right time of year—brown leaf slush on the roads, the smell of woodsmoke in the air, and a grey glaze of autumn over the sky. Mary told us what to look for: golden bells that bruised inky blue, smooth unslimy skin. Then we went crashing through the scrubby brush with plastic bags in hand, eyes glued to the ground. Under a tree Mary found a broken vibrator and a gay porn mag, the pages fused into a slab of wet cardboard by the rain. She found it hysterical, prodding at the pages with a stick trying to pry them open.

On the way back, I jumped in beside Jane in the sagging back seat. As we drove, our bodies slid over the shiny, cracked leather to meet in the middle. Our hands touched, and an ember flared in my belly.

Later, tripping, the three of us ran through the wild night, weaving through the coloured lights. Time not flowing anymore, but each moment shifting out of itself and into the next, a series of transformations, flowerings. We found a playground in the yard of a church and played on the swings like kids, in the streetlight shadow cast by a row of cypress trees. Syringes littered the dark corners beneath the eaves of the church.

We drifted to the Esplanade Hotel, where a grunge band thrashed their guitars and filled the air with the fuzz of industrial-strength distortion. I melted through the crowd, dripped over a three-dimensional surface of bodies. I was falling but somehow still walking, still talking, ordering a pot at the bar with words I shaped and bit out of plasticine. I stood side by side with Jane in the crush, watching the band. Her body was pressed into mine, and slowly, ever so slowly, like a twining creeper, my fingers curled into hers. When the band finished playing the crowd thinned and a space opened between our bodies. Her fingers slipped out of my hand. Mary had disappeared in the crowd and I took my chance.

Let's go out on the pier, I said.

So we ran out over the footbridge and into the weight of wind that pressed against us from the sea. The city glittered around the black gulf of the bay. Waves crumpled onto the sand. We kept running, laughing and wheezing, out onto the unlit breakwater where the waves crashed and sucked, and rats and crabs scuttled between the bluestone boulders. I led her down tentatively among the rocks until the light from the city was blocked out by the bulk of the sea-wall. We sat together on a boulder. It was cold and stark here where the city petered out and surrendered to the corrosive tide, the crust of salt and sea-life. But for the first time we were truly alone together.

She sat with her arms around her knees, shivering a little. It's cold, she said.

I was waiting for a sign from her, then I would turn and lift up her chin, and I would put my mouth on hers. Her lips and her tongue would be soft and hot enough to melt me. Surely she wouldn't be sitting here if she didn't expect me to do that. She'd held my hand in the pub. But I wasn't sure, not one hundred percent sure. Maybe I was just afraid she'd recoil as if she'd never dreamt of such a thing, as if the only reason she was there was because she'd never in a thousand years imagined I would try.

The wind blew up harder and I began to shiver too. I moved slightly towards her, put a hand behind her on the rock without touching her. Saying something lame to cover the gesture, make it seem casual. She was close, the bow of her lips mirroring the shape of the moon, her face almost insufferably lovely. It was a bright, night-burning thing.

Then a wave slapped into the rocks below, throwing up a chilly spray of brine.

Uggh, said Jane. That is bloody freezing! She pulled away and got to her feet.

Wait!

But she was already picking her way over the rocks to the path. On the pier, I saw a figure coming to meet us. It was Mary. As soon as they recognised one another, the two girls ran into a shrieking embrace. I watched from thirty metres away in the dark between the lights as Mary's plump, bangly arms encircled Jane's back. Just for an instant, Mary's eyes met mine, and I thought I saw in them the briefest flash of triumph.

A week later, I was passing Jane's doorway in the morning when I heard a giggle. I thought she and Mary must be mucking about again. The door was open a few inches, not enough for me to see the bed, but there was a crack between the door and its hinges, and I pressed my eye against it. On the bed I saw a mess of sheets, two bent knees, and between them a white arse with a long hairy crack, two thin legs stretched out. There was no movement. Then as I watched the buttocks squeezed. They slowly pulsed, pressed forward into her flesh like a slug. It was CD-man, I knew it.

I didn't see her again till later that evening when the two came out of her room. They were laughing together. His arm went round her waist.

In the living room Mary sat on the couch. She looked small and lost in the empty expanse of the sofa, the carpet around her feet littered with shreds of dope and tobacco, filters, rollie-papers, a mulling bowl and scissors. Her hands were wrapped around a bong, a plug of white smoke still caught in its throat. Her face was ghostly, almost translucent in the electric light.

You want one? she said.

I took it. Then another, and another. She poured me a tumbler of Southern Comfort and coke that was more booze than soft drink, and I downed it in one.

I told you she'd never go for you, said Mary. You just don't have what she wants. She wants a man, not a boy. You should have listened to me, then you wouldn't have got hurt…

She wouldn't stop talking and the room wouldn't stand still. Her face swam and bloated. I couldn't help myself. I began to cry, put my face in my hands. Like a stupid little kid. Mary reached out and touched me. Her hand was dry and cold.

It's not fair is it? she said. Then she took my wrist. Come with me.

I'd never been in her room before. It was dark, just the one candle throwing exaggerated shadows of the things on her mantelpiece. Black beads hanging in the window like a spider's web. I sat next to her on the bed. She wasn't a pretty girl, Mary. Her body was doughy and shapeless, but there was a hard line to her jaw, as if a tough life ahead were already rising up inside her and announcing itself in her face.

We tried, but it was no use, each of us straining to kiss the same mirage somewhere beyond the other's face. I kneaded her breast for a bit and she fumbled in my groin. Then it just petered out. We weren't even embarrassed. Just defeated. Across the room I saw she'd started a new painting: black vulva-woman. Even through the clumsy, misbegotten technique I could see it was Jane. Jane with a vulva like a hibiscus full of shark's teeth.

Do you love her too? I said.

Don't be stupid, she said. She took a small parcel of foil out of a drawer. You don't love her.

Inside the foil was a little pile of dirty grey snow, like something winter forgot to melt. I watched as she tipped it into a spoonful of water, held it over the candle flame. The snowflakes vanishing one by one. Then she expertly drew the fluid up into the syringe.

You wanna try?

I shook my head.

Go on, she said. It will make you feel better. Better than better. Trust me. It's the one thing better than love.

She tied a t-shirt round her bicep, pulled it tight. Her veins stood up like blue earthworms.

When the needle went in, she drew back the plunger and a little crimson bloom, a poppy of blood pulsed into the chamber.

Ah, said Mary, smiling beatifically. See that? The tornado. We call that the tornado.

I looked at it hanging there like a tiny jellyfish, so exquisite. A remote nebula, an A-bomb cloud in perfect miniature.

Isn't it pretty? she said.

The Thief

Loneliness and freedom are an amalgam that hardens with age. But as Julian Scholl drove down the Hume in '67, that lesson was far ahead of him. Leaving still had a salt-air tang about it back then, a salutary, purifying edge. It wasn't Sun Ra's *Atlantis* or Sergeant Pepper's that he remembered from that year, but *A Whiter Shade of Pale*, an accompaniment to the moment so perfect it just had to be a sign. Driving into a slice of late sun, that Bach-inspired organ solo chilled the fields with its beauty and he felt as if he were balanced on the crest of a wave, rushing headlong into a brilliant future, suspended between all he must become, and all that he must sadly leave behind. He slung his elbow in the open window, the cigarette between his fingers eating away in the gushing wind, and sang along at the top of his voice: *And so it was that later, as the miller told his tale, that her face, at first just ghostly, turned a whiter shade of pale.*

It was Hanna's pale face he was thinking of, bouncing and shaking in the rear-vision mirror as he'd driven down the grassy drive only an hour before, the salt of her tears on his lip. It was already late afternoon, the sun burning on his cheek and the breeze through the open window warm and smelling of wisteria and exhaust. He'd forced the gear lever into second and caught a last glimpse of her turning and walking back towards the house. Then he'd faced the road that climbed ahead of him, still hot enough from the dying day that at the crest of the hill a puddle of sky leaked into the bitumen, evaporating as he approached.

Julian had met Hanna eighteen months before, when she'd been living in a caravan up in Mullum with his old schoolmate, Dave who was building his mud-brick dream by infinitesimal degrees. But the rain, the ticks, the irrepressible vegetation, were winning the battle. Dave was getting desperate. He called Julian long-distance from a phone booth in Byron. 'Man, you gotta come up here,' he said. 'Paradise. You help me pack and stack bricks for a few days and you can have as much ganja as you can stuff in a bread-bag. Fair deal?' Dave had a couple of hundred plants growing up in the rainforest somewhere he wasn't letting on. The truth was Julian could take or leave the pot, but somehow conversations with Dave always led to him saying 'yes' to something or other.

It must have sounded idyllic to Hanna back in her parents' house in Ryde when Dave had painted the picture for her in his laconic-poetic way: three acres of unspoilt forest, a couple of kelpies, a night sky brimming over with stars. Escape from the stifling suburbs and a chance for a genuine piece of the counterculture. But one look at the brittle, desperate way she swatted the mosquitoes from her arms, and Julian knew she was coming apart, she was ripe to fall off the tree.

Not that he had designs. It was just that everything up here seemed to have its own uncivilised plans. Something to do with the encroaching wildness of the rainforest. Or maybe it was just the marijuana, the way it numbed the words in his head, dulled his limbs, and things just happened, unfolded like flowers following their own blind logic. In the night they made a fire and Dave strummed Dylan on his deadbeat nylon string, his rough rendition of *Like a Rolling Stone* still affecting enough out there in the stoned, portentous night to raise the hair on Julian's neck. The blackness outside the radiance of the firelight was total. When he walked away to take a piss and heard the stirring of the rainforest, saw the pale starlight on the dew, it was almost a surprise to find the world still existed.

He played jazz for them on his guitar. *Nature Boy, All The Things You Are, Autumn Leaves.* Dave closed his eyes, his face lost, while Hanna's shone limpid in the firelight, rapt. Later, as he lay in his tent, he heard a shuffle outside, someone fumbling with the zip. For a moment Julian's heart pounded with a city boy's bush paranoia, but it was Hanna slipping through the slit. Her teeth were chattering, the skin on her arms hard with cold, but when she took his hand and put it beneath her nightshirt, her breasts were warm.

'Dave,' he said, but she shooshed him: 'Don't wake him up.' When she kissed him, it left a lingering taste in his mouth, something acrid and aromatic, like a smear of incense on his tongue.

'I want to go back to Sydney,' she said.

'I know.'

'Tonight.'

A long, long silence. She kept pressing his hand against her breast, like some kind of covenant. Her desperation, her trust affected him. 'Okay,' he said at last. 'Okay.'

She made love to him single-mindedly, astride him in the dark, working her way towards her release with a silent, inward concentration that left him feeling almost incidental—a mere intersection between her body and its pleasure—and yet it was beautiful, strange, tender. Afterwards, he wrapped her in his blanket and she stood barefoot in the wet grass, while he quietly worked the pegs out of the earth in the dark, carefully folded up his tent. When he turned the ignition in the van the noise of the engine was like hell breaking loose. He switched on the headlights and reversed hard, panicking. In the glare, the caravan looked like a set in a play, marooned on the stage, its windows full of black. It shrank away from them. As they reached the road and the headlights swung off, they just caught the figure of a naked man breaking from the door, mouth open in a shout, running like a pale flame before the night extinguished it.

So it was he stole her and took her back to Sydney, where they shacked up in an old, run-down weatherboard in Balmain. They were broke, everything they owned scavenged from somewhere. An orange crate for a dinner table, a fifty-cent op-shop lamp by the bedside, an armchair by the window rescued from someone's nature strip. Apart from his kombi, he had just the one prized, valuable possession: his 1954 Gibson L5. He busked street corners for small change, played in clubs on quiet nights for a pittance, drew the dole. Hanna had no work at all, except her own project to transform the overgrown backyard into a vegie garden. She barely had the money for seeds, so she sneaked baby lettuces, tomato plants, whatever she could get away with from an Italian neighbour's garden, carrying them off under her coat with the exaggerated, casual walk of the shoplifter.

He was never sure whether their relationship was testament to the randomness of human relationships, or the reverse: the mysterious working of fate—for only one or the other seemed capable of explaining their unlikely union. Their difference was never more evident than when they held hands. Hers were small, white: little practical implements made for planting and picking and tending. Extensions of a simple, docile heart. Whereas his hands were elongated and bird-like, the long palms a mesh of complicated trajectories. Hands made for the abstractions of jazz, he supposed. Hanna had a little book on palm reading. She found the marks of three children in both their hands, scored on the side like notches in a belt. His head line was strong, his heart line faint and broken, she said. Which to him sounded convenient, like code for things she was always trying to convince him of anyway. But to him, the message in their hands needed no book to translate: they were utterly different people.

At night she curled against his body, like an animal: a wolf-cub or something less fierce, a rabbit or a lamb maybe. She radiated heat, clung to him in her sleep, so he had to gently prise her fingers from his chin or his hair, whatever she'd got hold of. When he freed himself she didn't wake but still fumbled for him, a blind person searching for something lost. She'd make little noises, then the restlessness would ebb away as she sank back into the still depths of her dreaming. It was in those moments he felt most able to love her. Not because of her need for him—he could see it was nothing but instinct in her, this clumsy groping for security. She'd done it the first night they slept together in that bed, when they were both more or less strangers to one another. No doubt she'd done it to Dave. It was no more personal than a plant's turning towards the sun. And yet it struck an ache into his chest to see her like that: so vulnerable, as if he were seeing the naked centre of her being, reaching out of its aloneness.

Julian never felt that Hanna really understood his passion for jazz, as much as she'd fallen for the musician that night in front of the fire. She could be swept up in the romance of the performance, but she was disillusioned to see all the work behind it. The repetition, the tedious scales, the painstaking hours copying out Wes Montgomery solos one little phrase at a time. She was stunned by it, irritated even. Is it really all worth it? she asked him, genuinely puzzled. She'd only ever seen the completed arches of music, never the structures underneath that had to be pulled away for the miracle of effortlessness to stand. She found it hard to leave him be. She'd come in while he was practising and stand there behind him, sometimes touch him, run her hand through his hair. Early on, he gave in to her; he'd lay down the guitar and relax against the soft brace of her belly. She'd lift his lips up to hers, and they would make love in the leisurely afternoon. But slowly he came to resent her. She was like a cat that has to jump on the newspaper, always interposing herself into the path of his attention. He learnt to ignore her, playing on in spite of the shadow of need lurking behind him until she would at last withdraw, quietly closing the door behind her.

Then she would be cold to him, and he would accuse her of being a child, and then he'd bring in the Buddhist philosophy he'd been reading.

   FAULT LINES

Attachment and aversion are the faults that bind you to the wheel of karma, he explained patiently. She should meditate on her samsaras. There should be nothing in your life you can't walk away from, he said. Only then can you really be free.

One rainy night he heard a knock on the door. It was after two a.m., according to the faint dots on his watch, and Hanna was fast asleep. At first he thought he'd dreamt it, but then it came again, a sharp rapping through the ceaseless applause of the rain. He pulled on his jeans, a t-shirt and stumbled to the door. On the doorstep a dishevelled drunk, soaked to the skin, beer bottle in hand.

'Fuck off,' he said, and went to slam the door, but the man had already got a foot in the way, deceptively fast.

'Asnot nice, Julian, 'snot nice at all.'

He recoiled at his name, looked closer at the face beneath the plastered, dripping hair.

'Dave!'

'Asright, your old mate, Davo. Bes' buddies, right?'

Julian's hand on the doorframe shook, but he steadied it.

'We were never best buddies, Dave.'

Dave's stare was unfocussed and woozy, but full of hate. Julian's heart whanged in his chest, his fist tightened, ready for a drunken haymaker, but instead his old friend deflated, his eyes fell, the aggression all sham. He fished about in the pocket of his coat, extracted a limp and sorry joint, which he then tried to light, thumbing useless flashes from the flint of his Bic.

'You got a light?'

'Go away, Dave.'

'C'mon man, just let me see her.' He tried to look past Julian into the hallway.

'It's two in the morning. She's asleep.'

'Please. I just ... need to see her, okay? Just once, then ...' He reeled, waved the damp spliff about as if magicking himself away. 'Gone. Never to darken your ... fucken door. Again. Okay?'

Julian didn't reply.

'Please...' A thick sob escaped from his chest.

Julian kept blocking the door, unmoved, immovable.

More sobs. 'But why? Why did you do it, man? Me and Hanna, we were happy together. We were ... fucken great, you know?'

'Bullshit. She hated it there. You couldn't see that?'

'Asnot true. When we finished the house ...' He petered out.

'Forget it. If it hadn't been me, would've been someone else. She didn't love you.'

That made Dave crumple in the middle, like some critical scaffold had been pulled out of him. He leaned against the wall and wept.

Julian tried to close the door, but Dave grabbed the edge.

'And you,' he spat.

'What?'

'Do you love her?'

He prised Dave's fingers from the wood.

'Well do you, mister fucken iceman? At least answer that.'

He shut the door in Dave's sozzled, dripping face, turned, and there was Hanna standing in her nightie in the doorway of the bedroom, sleepy, mussed and shivering, arms clutched round her breasts for warmth. Dave hammered on the door with his fist. 'Well do you?'

'Who's that?' said Hanna.

'Some drunken idiot. It's okay. He's leaving now.'

'Is that Dave? What's he doing? Why's he saying that?'

'Come on, he's pissed. Let's go back to bed.'

'Do you, you fucker?'

'What does he mean?' she said. Julian took her shoulder and she let herself be led, childlike in her sleepiness, but her brow was troubled and she cast a last glance at the door as Julian steered her away into the bedroom.

Elsewhere they called it the Summer of Love, but between them a silence opened, crept into the spaces of the house like a colourless, odourless gas, even while they enacted an unchanged intimacy. A restlessness crawled under Julian's skin, an itch for wind and loneliness and sunburn. When he played his guitar it was all diminished scales, edgy and unresolved, evading the root and rolling on. As he lay in Hanna's arms, the mosquitoes whining in the dark and the moon making a slick of light on his chest, he felt her slipping off him, like a drowning person slipping from a rock. With every inhalation of the redolent summer air he felt he was growing bigger, too big for her, this pretty, good-natured girl from Ryde. Her arms were slipping off his gigantic chest.

He told her he was leaving. He was going to Melbourne, where he'd heard the jazz scene was going off. In the end it was easy to do. His heart was heavy but his spirit light. He had so little stuff, all he needed to do was throw his clothes in a bag, pack his music and his books into a few boxes, pick up his guitar. Hanna watched him, her face puffy and ruined with sorrow. 'Why?' she kept asking. 'What have I done wrong?'

He put his guitar into the back of the kombi, turned to her. That was it, he was packed. With everything in the van he felt the last root tearing free. He was ready to fly. She came into his arms and he held her in a loose, empty embrace while she shuddered. She lifted her face to kiss him saltily. Her kiss aroused him, but not for her, not really. He was hard for whatever lay down that highway, turned on by the act of leaving, this leaping into flight.

He would regret throwing away the letter he received from Hanna two months after he left, telling him she was pregnant. He saw only the trap, never guessed at the longing he'd have one day just to know the child's name. But right then, as he sang along to Procol Harum and shielded his eyes against the brilliance of the sun, against the dazzling light of his possibilities, his freedom and his loneliness were light as air, as wild and beautiful as youth. Driving on after sunset, he thought of the night he stole Hanna, and it seemed to him he was stealing something again, though he wasn't sure what. The guilt and the thrill were the same, though the seat beside him was empty this time. He was just stealing himself. The white line of the road unspooled out of a great and pregnant darkness. He was quite certain it was leading somewhere, that its endless snaking dance encoded some deep purpose. He leaned forward into the dark, his body tight with impatience. And all around, the flat and barren fields lay unseen and unchanging, their silence only briefly ruffled by the van that rushed through them, chasing its own light.

Salt

When Norma stopped driving, she had reached the edge of the moon —or so it appeared through the windscreen of Jack's Hiace as she sat there, shocked by the sudden silence. She stepped out of the car and, looking up, breathed in a cold lungful of stars. The only sounds she could detect in that whole immensity were those she had brought with her: the sound of her own life moving through her, breath and blood, and the car ticking as its heat bled away into the night. She walked to the edge of the luminous expanse that lay ahead in the moonlight and crouched down to crumble the white rime between her fingers. She touched the crystals against her tongue and felt them burn and melt, her mouth flooding with saliva. And then she walked and then she ran, out onto the great emptiness of Lake Torrens, and kept running with her eyes closed until her heart hurt from pounding and her breath rang harsh in her ears. When she opened her eyes she could no longer find Jack's car in the dark; she had lost all reference points. She had come as far as she could. So she laid herself out on the salt, face to the silent stars, and prepared herself for the tide of pain that was already rising in her bones.

Nine months earlier, in a room a thousand miles east, Norma's father Jack lay in an upstairs bedroom. It was late summer and the room stank, a gagging combination of Jack's sick sweat, antiseptic, faeces and something else that Norma assumed was the cancer. She had opened the one small window as wide as it would go, but it gave no relief, either from the smell or the heat. The landscape of red tin roofs shimmered liquid.

Jack had a buzzer installed beside his bed so that he could summon Norma whenever he needed her. Inevitably it was for some repulsive chore: to hold a wad of tissues in front of his mouth while he half coughed, half puked great gobs of blood-blackened phlegm, or to remove his bedpan, swilling with watery shit so evil-smelling she nearly retched as she tipped it down the toilet. She, who had spent twenty years changing bedpans. His humiliation made him hate her. She could see the baleful fervour in his eyes as they followed her over the oxygen mask. He no longer had the breath to yell, but to have his abuse whispered into her ear from six inches away, his hand clawing her arm and spittle on his lips, was somehow worse. She recoiled from the vile intimacy of it.

'Kill that...' he wheezed.

'What was that?'

'Kill that ...' his face purpled with rage and effort ' ... FLY!'

A blowfly had come in through the window, and was now whirling around the room, tap-tap-tapping the walls with its tiny weight. She took up a towel from the end of the bed and swatted at it, missing a few times before it found the aperture of the window again and disappeared into the baking heat outside.

'Closethefuckingwindow,' said Jack.

The cancer that had started in his lungs had cauliflowered through his body, every scan revealing some new cluster of florets blossoming in the viscera. The doctors had sent him home to die with a morphine pump he could control himself, pressing a button whenever he needed to top up the dose. She knew his oncologist from her nursing days. A tired man with the eyes of a bloodhound, he was sympathetic to her fears, promised her, with meaningful emphasis, that the morphine would be 'as plentiful as needed'. But Jack's body was tough; its roots twined deep into life and the disease had one hell of a job prying him loose of it. It coiled and knotted and the old man wore an expression of utter concentration as he battled the thing, locked in its unrelenting clinch.

Before he got his buzzer, he'd tormented her with his querulous cries of 'Normaaa!', repeated twenty times a day in exactly the same cadence. That now seemed preferable to the peremptory bark of that cursed buzzer. She felt the gut-clutch, the hot flush of stress almost before she registered the sound of it. He expected her to drop whatever she was doing instantly. Even then she was never quick enough. The first blast of demand would be followed by a second, a third, a series of stabs and jabs. Whole morse-code stanzas, elaborate one-note improvisations on the theme of *get your arse in here.* Sometimes he'd just lean on the damn thing; he could hear her labouring up the stairs—Christ knows she was no spring chicken herself, those stairs were a chore—but he'd still hold down the button until he saw her in the doorway.

How did it go wrong for you? she sometimes asked in her mind as she looked into those pale, hate-filled eyes. It seemed to her that there was a knot in him that every experience only drew tighter. Can the soul form a knot? And if it can, what can untie such a thing, how can it ever come loose? She wished she knew more about these things. She'd offered to move his bed into the sunroom so he could look out over the garden. He could watch the birds disporting in the bird-bath, see the wind move through the trees. He might live long enough to watch the jonquils that she'd planted come up. She imagined that when you are dying the beauty of such things would be focussed like sun through a magnifying glass. Perhaps the bright spot it made in your heart would sear, but who would not welcome a burn like that? Surely we all long to be purified, and with nothing more to come, no more errors or losses or compromises, the spring garden could have the last word, the final say on it all. Wouldn't anyone want that? Well, not Jack. He refused to be moved and when she tried to 'jolly him along', taking him by the arm, he actually struck out at her as if she were trying to lure him into some form of involuntary euthanasia. So he stayed in his dark, musty room with its mouldy walls and its sweet stink of cancer. Go ahead, she thought, eat up your own misery. Knock yourself out. She sat on the side of his bed and tried to get a few spoonfuls of pureed vegetables into his mouth, but he was like an infant, with the added faculty of cunning. After long exhortations, he finally opened his mouth for the spoon then spat the stuff out in a spray all down his front, knowing she would have to clean up every spot. She could have cried. She could have killed him.

As summer faded, she watched his pain grow and, in spite of everything, felt pity for him. His back arched and his eyes focussed on some point in inner space beyond anyone's reach, the sweat streaming off his face. What territories of pain he was traversing she could not imagine. He'd claw for the button on his morphine machine and she'd watch his pupils contract and his body ease back down into the embrace of the bed.

One night Helen rang from Alice Springs, where she worked on a remote Aboriginal community teaching the poor little mites to read and write. Norma had never visited, but she almost thought she could hear the landscape in Helen's voice—had her accent flattened and broadened? She sounded tough and relaxed, dusty, sunburned. She sounded free. In her mind Norma saw the immense, quiet desert sinking into dark, cockatoos crossing the vast light of dusk, and her heart ached in her chest.

'So how's Dad?' Helen asked. What she meant of course was how long? Helen—ever the organised one—wanted to get an idea of when she'd have to buy a flight.

Norma let out a long exhalation. 'I have no idea. He needs the oxygen more. He's weaker than he was. But it's so slow, Helen, I can't tell you.'

The phone was silent for a long time. 'Won't go down without a fight, will he?'

'Stubborn as a Mallee bull.'

Then the talk turned to medications and metastases and all the rest, and Norma switched into nurse mode, a sort of autopilot, speaking in a rush. She was holding herself tight as a pillar in the middle of the living room and all this medical stuff was tumbling out of her mouth, though it wasn't what she really wanted to say. Helen listened, or perhaps she didn't. She mm-hmmed at the appropriate points.

And then: zzzzzzzzzzzzzzzzzzzzzzzzzzzzzz!! A cattle prod to Norma's kidneys.

'What's that noise?' her sister asked.

Norma felt tears pricking, and took a moment to control the shake that threatened to disturb the efficient calm of her voice. 'Oh, that's him. He wants something.'

zzzzzzzzz!! zzzzzzzzzz!! zzzz!! zzzzzzzzzzzzzzzzzzzzzzzz!!

'I guess you'd better go. Thanks for the update.' Helen paused. 'So how are you going, anyway?'

That's what Norma had been waiting for, that little question. Instead of all that stuff about Jack's cancer, she'd really just wanted to scream I'm dying here, I don't know how much longer I can take his abuse and the stink and the day after day after day I'm not coping not coping at all please help me ...

But Jack was hammering the buzzer and Helen was being polite. She didn't want to know that her big sis was an emotional basket case.

'Oh, you know, soldiering on,' Norma said.

'That's good. I honestly don't know how you put up with him. You know we all appreciate it.' By which she meant she and Norma's other three siblings, who were, if you summed the distances, collectively as far away as the moon, probably.

zzzzzzzzzzzzzzzzzzzzzzzzz!! zzzz!! zzzzzzzzzzzzzzzzzzzzzzzzzzzzzzzzzzzzzzzzz zzzzzzzzzzzzzzz!!

'ALRIGHT!' she shouted and hung up the phone. She went upstairs and the sallow illumination of the forty-watt Osram was like the light in a bad dream. She was displaced into some other century or world. She became unreal to herself and wouldn't have been surprised to discover she was a ghost living in a repetitive purgatory of her own making, like in that film *The Others*.

The day after, Norma had the vials for Jack's pump in her hand when the thought crossed her mind—what would it be like? She stopped, right in the middle of the room and looked down at the two little glass tears in the palm of her hand. The room spun for a moment and she had the dizzy sensation that she was rushing over a precipice. Then she shook herself and pushed the thought away. She would never do something like that.

But a few days later she did. Taking the medicine from the shelf she felt the same emotion as a child stealing chocolate from the corner shop. Norma couldn't believe she was doing it, how terrifying and exciting it was. She went down to the kitchen and the very light seemed diamond-cut, sharp-edged with adrenalin. Her heart was beating so hard her ribs shook, but her hand was steady as she prepared the syringe, flicked her nail against the plastic, squeezed out a little drop. She would make an exceptionally professional junkie, she thought. No septicaemia or collapsed veins for her, no sir. She plumped up a vein with a tea-towel tourniquet and shot the stuff home before she had time to think twice.

And oh dear god the sweet release as those opioid molecules sleeted through her blood, buried her in a blizzard of painlessness. She melted into a chair and the pleasure came down on her with an oceanic weight. The clock kept quietly ticking over the fridge and here she was, at the bottom of the universe where nothing could touch her. She needed to lie down, but the walk to the bedroom was too much, so she slipped like a dropped scarf to the lino. The cold floor was as comfortable as a feather bed. She closed her eyes, and, like the Cheshire Cat, the rest of her faded away—she became nothing but one immense smile.

Afterwards she realised what a stupid, stupid mistake she had made. She could have spat on herself she was so disgusted. Words were not vile enough to describe her. What was she thinking? She was no ignorant, screwed-up kid. She knew what addiction was about. She knew the physiology of it, for Christ's sake. She knew the price. But what could she do now? Knowing that each of those vials on the shelf contained a cosmic orgy of relief. How do you get the genie back in that bottle? Oh, the sick, excited feeling when she thought about those damn vials. It reminded her of something. It was exactly the same as something else she'd experienced a long, long time ago. She realised what it was as she was putting out the washing one day: love, first love. Yes, that was it exactly.

Winter blew in, scattering dead leaves and ragged clouds over the town, driving the birds before it. The air felt cold and full of wet, but still no rain came except random spats of oversized drops, like someone wringing out a wet dish cloth over the roof. On Sunday at church the talk was all of survival, and everyone bowed their heads to pray for rain, but Norma felt like a crow among doves; she was praying only for Jack's death. How could this go on? She'd rung every agency she could think of, but all she could get was a relieving nurse one day a fortnight—that was all she was 'eligible' for.

She stole his morphine again not long after that. She'd been lying awake again, exhausted but unable to sleep, and at some point she heard the quiet shift of night into morning. Thinking of the day ahead she felt an arid despair. The tears she might have shed had dried up inside her. She was as drought-stricken and saline as the town, she was withered inside. She got up and pulled on her dressing-gown and went down the hall to Jack's room. She shook the box into her palm, meaning to take two like last time—twenty mils should do the trick—but five fell into her hand, and she found her fingers closing over them. Fifty mils—she'd still be okay. She went back to bed, and by the light of the moon in her window, drew their contents one by one up into the syringe. She felt the weight of the cylinder as she held it up, needle glinting in the light, and noticed she was wet between her legs. There was a moment of hot, dirty shame before she found the vein and the rush came, obliterating everything.

When the itching started the next day, she noted it with some professional surprise. She had not expected the symptoms so soon.

The jonquils had come up. Oh, how beautiful they are, Norma thought. I knew they would be. Through her dull somnolence she watched their bright heads tossing in the wind that came scouring through the garden, and vaguely feared for their petals. The clothesline spun aimlessly. She was a little clumsy opening the boxes and quite a few of the vials spilled off the table and rolled on the floor.

When she came into his room and took his hand, Jack's head turned. Mum, he whispered, Mum is that you? She put her hand on his forehead and said, Yes, Jack it's me, it's okay, it's going to be okay.

She was numb right through, her body just a deadweight. But her cheeks were wet. Salt ran into her mouth.

Mum, what is happening to me?

It's okay.

While the wind thrummed in the windowpane, she emptied the first syringe into his arm.

It's okay.

His head rolled over to watch his own arm as one by one she pushed in the needles. He looked startled.

It's okay.

His eyes grew faraway and his pupils shrank to stars in negative. She waited, not looking at him, but gazing into the white patch of sky framed in the window. After a time she could not have measured, she realised she was alone in the room, so she went downstairs to make the necessary calls.

She'd kept one box, just one, to get her through the arrangements and the funeral and the siblings flying in and departing before the things that needed to be said could be. And then she locked up the house forever, closing the door on all its ghosts, and got into Jack's car. The last vial was used up. She took a deep breath and started to drive, following the semitrailers west out of town, through the sun that flashed between the trees, and onwards towards the great emptiness that lay ahead.

The Magpie

From the grassy verge of the oval Ewen watches as the football arcs high into the cold sunlight. At the top of its flight it hovers momentarily in the clear, wintry blue. Far below, the pack is already anticipating its descent, converging on the far end of its parabola. But as it falters and begins to accelerate downwards, Ewen's eyes remain fixed on that point at the top of its arc where it seems to pause. He imagines he could build a shelf up there in the air to catch the ball and hold it there. He pictures the children below, their upturned faces beginning to frown, their extended arms sagging to their sides, and the ball suspended in the air, like a little muddy leather moon. *I'm never coming down again.* In the end they'd disperse, disappointed, cheated of the thudding satisfaction of the mark. But Ewen would stay. He'd still be there when the magpies swooped beneath it, dog-fighting blackbirds over the empty, trampled oval.

After the game, Richard Sterling, one of Ewen's schoolmates, wanders up to where he is sitting, staging a swordfight on his skinny knees with two tiny twigs. His right hand is the goody, but the left hand is putting up quite a fight.

'Hey, Ewen,' Richard drawls, 'whatcha up to?'

'Nothing,' he replies, dropping the twigs. 'Just watching the game.'

'Why don't you join in some time?' But he's not saying it to be nice. He's just reminding Ewen of what they both know, which is that Ewen is crap at football. He's unco, always the last kid to be picked, unless Bruce Duhic is in the line-up, but that's no consolation, because Duhic's a mongoloid. The sun's right behind where Richard is standing, and Ewen blinks up at him, sheltering his eyes against the brilliance with his hand. 'You doing anything now?' Richard asks him.

'No.'

'Why don't you come round to my place? I've got something to show you.'

'What is it?'

'It's a secret. But I'll let you see if you come round.'

'Go on, tell me, please.'

'Well, if you don't want to that's fine. I'll ask Warren.' He makes to walk off, a few phony steps.

'No, no, I do,' says Ewen, jumping up. The backs of his knees hurt as he straightens them, they've been bent up so long in the cold.

Ewen trails behind Richard as they cut across the oval and down the embankment at the back to where there's a gap in the fence. It's a shortcut through the school to Richard's street. Ewen picks up a springy stick from under a wattle tree, swings it in front of him as he walks. There's a washed-out fragment of moon hanging in the blue morning sky.

'My dad says that God lives on the moon,' he confides to Richard's back.

'That's rubbish.'

'Is not.'

'There's no such thing as God, so how can he live on the moon?'

'There is! He's got a big castle on the moon with a telescope, and he watches everything that goes on. That's why he made the moon. So he'd have somewhere to watch from.'

'That's stupid. I can prove it.'

'Can not.'

'Can so. I've got a telescope at home. If God was up there, you'd be able to see him. But you can't. 'Cos there's nothing up there except craters.

I'll show you when you get to my place. And anyway, why didn't the astronauts see him when they went to the moon?'

'He was probably on the other side.'

'Your dad's a retard.'

Ewen feels tears of rage pricking at the back of his eyeballs. He knows he'll cry if he tries to say anything, so he keeps his mouth shut. He doesn't want to look through Richard's stupid telescope.

Richard lives in a big house right at the bottom of Melaleuca Road. All the houses down there are big, double-storey buildings, their over-sized brown walls jostling one another as if they've outgrown the land they sit on. Richard's house even has an incomplete third storey, a bare wood skeleton with blue tarpaulin flapping between its naked ribs. Richard is forever describing the wonders it will contain: pool tables and colour televisions and a bar full of as much Coke as you can drink. Ewen can't believe it will ever be finished. It seems to have been in the same gutted condition forever.

He's never quite sure about visiting Richard's house. There's a funny smell that makes him feel nervous. But he likes Richard's mum. She fixes him milkshakes in their make-a-shake, and gives him icy poles from the freezer. At home, the only freezer they have is just a shelf inside the fridge, permanently gummed up with ice. But the Sterlings' freezer is like a whole separate fridge. Cold, white smoke flows out of it and onto the floor when Mrs Sterling opens the lid to get Ewen an Icy-pole.

'There you go, darling,' she'll say. Ewen likes it when she says that. He also likes it when she plants those big, sloppy, lipsticky kisses on his cheek, even though it's embarrassing. Ewen's mother hardly ever calls him darling, and when she kisses him, her lips are dry and absent.

Mrs Sterling is thin and her skin is brown and crinkles like crepe paper around her eyes when she smiles. She always wears white socks and sneakers and whenever Ewen sees her, she seems to be about to run out the door with a squash racquet in her hand. Her sandy blond hair is cut short like a boy's and her eyes, when you can see them, are blue like the marbles that bower birds collect. But often her eyes are hidden behind sunglasses as big as dinner plates. She smiles from behind them but sometimes her lips seem to tremble as if they are fragile and ready to break.

Mr Sterling is not often at home, but Ewen is scared of him. One time he saw him cutting up meat with an enormous cleaver in the kitchen, slamming the blade down between the bones and splitting the huge ribcage into thick, bloody steaks. Ewen was sure he was going to take off his own sausage-like fingers with every blow, but Richard told him that his dad used to be a butcher and never missed. The back of one of Mr Sterling's muscly calves is scarred by a vast crater, an indentation the size and shape of a flan tray. Ropes of scar tissue spread like creepers from the edges of the crater into the surrounding skin. Mr Sterling told him once that was where the doctors had 'taken their pound of flesh'. Ewen didn't know what that meant but he imagined them hacking a pound of meat out of his leg with cleavers, throwing the bloody mass on the scales and wrapping it in butcher's paper.

Richard leads Ewen down under the house to the garage. He fishes out a cardboard box from under a shelf. There are breathing holes cut in it. Richard holds the box out towards Ewen. 'Listen,' he says. Ewen puts his ear against the box and hears a thin, scrabbling noise from inside.

'What is it?' Ewen breathes, but Richard ignores the question, carries the box outside into the backyard. He sits down cross-legged in the grass, opens the box and tips its contents out onto the lawn.

Blinking in the sunlight is a tiny baby magpie.

'It fell out of the tree,' Richard says, giving it a little push from behind with his index finger. It falls forward helplessly.

'Don't,' says Ewen, crouching to scoop the tiny creature into his palm. Ewen loves magpies. Loves their early morning chortling, a joyous sound like the bubbling of a stream, loves their fierce black eyes and sharp, precise beaks. He doesn't even mind when they dive-bomb him on the way to school. It's the same fearless spirit that sees them drive off ravens twice their size. On spring mornings he steals mince from the fridge and goes out into the garden and calls to them. There's a family of magpies that lives high up in the stand of old stringybarks on Davis Court behind his house. He loves to see them streaking down through the slanting shadows cast by the eucalypts. They land on the lawn, perhaps in the shade where the grass is frosted a glaucous blue, or in the sun amid the gem-sparkle of the dew. Not minding the cold or the wet, he lies out flat, extending his hand with the mince on the tips of his fingers. Getting down low is the key to making them feel safe. The older female, the matriarch, is the boldest. She looks smart in her sleek black and whites. While the males stand back, dithering, she edges in close, her head turned to the side so she can fix Ewen with the shrewd bead of her eye. 'Come on, girl,' he whispers to her, not daring to move a muscle.

Then swiftly, confidently, but circumspectly, she swipes the meat from his hand, the tip of her beak delivering a sharp kiss to the pads of his fingertips. She hops away to a safe distance and throws her head back to let the tasty morsel slide down her throat. Ewen smears more meat on his fingers and puts out his hand again. She'll eat enough for herself, then take the rest away to her babies waiting up in the distant trees.

Ewen looks at the tiny, blind creature in the cage of his fingers. Its eyes are as small and black as caviar. Its wings lift up and down mechanically like a wind-up toy. The soft grey fluff that covers it seems poorly stuck on, and there are patches of bald, pink skin as if the job has not been completed. It weighs nothing, a poorly assembled creature of toothpicks and clockwork that might blow away in a stiff breeze. Ewen sees that there are mites of some description crawling over its skin. Deep down he knows the bird is dying.

Ewen sits down opposite Richard and places the feeble animal back on the grass between them.

'What are you feeding it?' he asks.

'Grass mainly.'

'Grass?'

'Yeah, don't magpies eat grass? That's what they seem to do all day—go around pecking at grass.'

'They're looking for worms.'

'Oh, right.'

'Maybe we should try to catch some worms now, and cut them up for it.'

'Gross. I don't want to cut up worms.'

'Well, it's going to die if you don't feed it.'

'Can't you see it's going to die anyway? Dad says that's what birds are like. They always die if you try to keep them.'

What the hell were you thinking of? Suddenly Mr Sterling's voice cuts across the yard, an ugly sound like the bark of the Doberman that lives on Horace Avenue. Ewen jumps, scared, and looks at Richard, expecting to see the same fear on his face. But instead his face is contorted into a kind of smile. Only it isn't a real smile, just a sort of twist of his mouth. He doesn't say anything. Instead he gives the bird another poke with his forefinger, causing it to fall forward on its chin again. 'It's suffering,' he says.

'Should we ask your mum or … dad to take it to the vet?' Ewen asks without conviction, knowing they can't possibly go inside the house.

How many times do I have to tell you to ask me? Are you fucking stupid or what? Mr Sterling's voice barks out again. It isn't the words that make ice run in Ewen's veins. It is the savage snarling, the baring of teeth. He has an image of Mr Sterling on all fours like a wolf, his lip curled back and his face contorted with viciousness.

'Are you fucking stupid or what?' Richard mimics the words in a mocking sing-song, that smile twisted onto his lips. Like it was a big joke. Then he looks straight at Ewen. 'We should kill it. It would be kinder to kill it.'

'I don't want to. I want to go home,' says Ewen.

'I thought you liked magpies.'

'I do.'

'Well, then you shouldn't let it suffer like this. You should kill it if you care about it.'

Something smashes in the house and Ewen flinches again. He looks at the house, but its windows just stare back blindly, reflecting the bright morning like Mrs Sterling's sunglasses.

Piss off, you cunt.

'Piss off, you cunt,' echoes Richard under his breath. Then he picks up a big stick. 'Here,' he says. 'You can use this.'

Ewen takes the stick, then tries to give it back. 'You do it,' he says. 'I don't want to.'

'Are you chicken?'

'No. I just don't want to.'

'Chicken. Bawk-bawk-bawk.' He flaps his elbows.

Don't look at me like that, you stupid bitch. Something else smashes.

'Don't look at me like that, you stupid bitch.'

'Stop it!' says Ewen.

'What?'

'I don't want to kill it.'

'Why do you want it to suffer? You have to kill it.'

Oh, very clever, Marcia. I suppose you think that's funny. Do you think this is funny too? There's another crashing noise.

'I suppose you think that's funny. Do you think this is funny too?'

'Stop it!' Ewen shouts. 'Stop doing that.' He lifts the stick and brings it down on the tiny fledgling. There is a soft crunching sound. Richard leans forward. His voice is excited. 'Look what you've done. You've broken its leg, and its wing.'

Ewen looks and sees that the bird's wing is twisted and crushed, and one of its legs is snapped like a matchstick, sticking out to the side. Its beak is opening and closing and a faint peeping noise is coming from its throat. Horrified, Ewen clubs it again. This time the stick strikes it in the middle of its back and there is a crunch as its spine and rib cage collapse. But still it won't die. A sticky rope of blood stretches from its beak to a blade of grass, and it goes on gasping, gasping, silently.

He hits it a third time, and a fourth, crushing its body nearly flat, and still its wings and head twitch. How could it be so hard to kill such a tiny, frail animal? Finally, with the fifth blow, he smashes its skull like an eggshell, and the bird stops moving. The grass is a crimson mess.

Ewen drops the stick and covers his face, the tears coming hot and fast. He doesn't want to cry in front of Richard, but he can't stop himself. Thick choking sobs wrack him. Behind his eyelids all he can see is the bird's uncomprehending eyes, its head stretching forward as it gasps for air with its shattered lungs, the string of blood in the grass.

'Why'd you go and do that?' he hears Richard say.

Ewen drops his fingers away from his face. 'What?'

Richard's face is accusing, nasty. 'Why'd you go and kill my bird?'

'You told me to.'

'Liar! Look what you've done. You've killed my bird.'

'It was sick. You told me I had to!' Ewen's head reels with confusion.

'You're the one who's sick. You're a murderer!' screams Richard, bubbles of spittle forming in the corners of his mouth.

Something snaps in Ewen's head, and blackness floods in like blood. He covers his ears and screams so he can't hear Richard's words, closes his eyes to blot out his savage, twisted face. He jumps up and runs down the side of the house. Richard is behind him, barking and barking as Ewen scrambles over the gate and flees down the drive.

He runs through the empty Saturday morning streets, his own sobbing chasing him like a ghost over his shoulder, the world swimming in his tears, runs all the way to the stand of stringybarks on Davis Court. Then he climbs. Up, up into the clean morning light. So high he can feel the tree flex and creak in the breeze. He sits there, far above the world, pulling his skinny bird-legs up to his chest. The moon gazes at him through the shuffling leaves, like an empty, scarred eye. The sound of lawnmowing drifts up from the suburban morning. The leaves whisper. Somewhere a magpie sings.

I'm never coming down again, he thinks. *I'm never coming down.*

Wasp's Nest

Sylvie had discovered wasps in her bathroom wall. More and more she'd found them, battering on the small frosted window or crawling in the tub. She pressed her ear to the wall and heard their awful pullulating industry. Once Alan would have dealt with something like that, but he was gone, so she had to do it herself. She found the place inside her cupboard where they crawled out and filled it with a can of Mortein. As she stood there trembling with horror, the sound in the wall grew feverish, and the dying wasps started tumbling out, then the maggots, half-formed wasp bodies writhing inside the glistening pulp. She closed the cupboard and walked away. When she showered the next day, the wall was silent.

Whenever she got off the tram at the corner of Spencer and Latrobe to visit the prison, and looked up at those high, serried windows, she experienced the same shudder. She imagined that if she were to put her ear to the prison wall she would hear the same quiet, terrifying chorus, the seethe of angry, confined men. She'd seen them in the visitors centre, the damage milking over the alarming blue of their eyes. Their arms were thin and raw, but hard as concrete, and every man who displeased them was a maggot.

At reception she put her belongings in a locker. Money, phones, keys, pens: everything was contraband beyond the first steel door—had some sinister connotation she, in her innocence, could never have imagined. When her name was called she waited for the door to buzz and let her through to the metal detectors and the first hit of that smell, that prison smell. Antiseptic and greasy beef casserole and metal, semen, sweat, fear. A thin, comfortless smell. Everything painted beige or grey, sterile yet ingrained with the smear of filthy hands that won't scrub out. She thought of hospitals; the same anxiety, the same aseptic corridors. Only here the patients were all men, and the doctors wore blue and were all built the same: fat behinds and forearms and walking with a handcuff swagger. The women no different. Like the one who took her aside into a stinking hot cubicle for a random strip search, jawing gum, her face set in lines of bored contempt.

Sylvie took one glance into the officer's eyes and could see the dull hate there. One hand on her baton, like a riot cop, and that black thing dangling around her neck, the duress alarm. Sylvie stood there, trembling in her underwear, intimacies she barely let Alan see.

Have to take those off too ma'am. Nothin' personal.

It was hot, so unbearably hot, and she was ashamed of the beads of sweat breaking out on her chest and upper lip. She couldn't do it, she really couldn't. But what would Alan say? If she didn't submit to the search they would throw her out and ban her. Guilty until proven uninteresting, trial by shame. The pressure of impossible alternatives was building in her throat, a horrific, almost irresistible urge to cry, but she told herself no, she mustn't. She absolutely wouldn't.

Look, dja wanna visit or doncha? Either make up your mind and go home or get it over with. 'Cos nicer lookin' old ladies'n you have brung in prohibited substances before and I haven't got all day.

Sylvie saw through her alright, through the pressed uniform that sat so stiffly on the brute's square shoulders. Through the officious lingo of 'prohibited substances', failed policewoman talk. You're no better than us, she thought. You're off the same street, and you probably kicked my kids at school.

The woman arched her eyebrows, mouth chewing, eyes cold and level. Sylvie thought she wouldn't be able to do what she had to, that she was going to suffocate in the heat, but then she remembered an old trick, something she learnt so long ago she forgot where. How to leave your body, how to make everything happen to a thing that isn't you, to somebody else, or nobody, just an actor in a movie. It's happening to an actor who, when it's over, will turn around and say, *How was that? How'd I do?*

So she closed her eyes and did what she was told and the woman shone a torch up her anus, quick and businesslike.

Saying believe me I don't do this for fun.

In the visitors centre she scanned the room, Alan was sitting hunched at the plastic table, so shrunken she hardly recognised him. She was looking for the big strong mechanic she'd married, who'd so often bragged about the dodgy parts dealers he'd bested at the garage—not this frightened old man with his unshaven cheeks and edgy, fast-moving eyes. It was noisy and heckling in there, the kids bored and screaming while their parents huddled, bracketing their snatched intimacy with their backs and trying to grope one another out of sight of the officers. Alan stood and pulled out a chair for her—that was him all over, always polite, knew how to treat a lady. It was why she married him, that old-fashioned courtesy. A true gentleman, she always said. A gentleman at a time when her body and soul thirsted for gentleness like water. The bruises had faded, the bones mended, but after she escaped her first marriage she still suffered a terrible tenderness in her skin. A harsh word made her shake, the abrasion of a doorway hurt like a blow, even the hard light of summer assaulted her and had her wearing her dark glasses again, hiding in them like a shellfish. She had thought she could never bear to let a man touch her again. But then there had been Alan, courting her with flowers, the old-fashioned way.

And she'd told him. She'd said to him that if his intentions weren't honourable then he could forget it right away; she wasn't like that. Of course, she knew she was damaged goods and was lucky to have him at all, someone to take her to the pokies on a Saturday night, or drive her to Target when she needed a new pair of shoes. But it had given her such pleasure playing the role of someone she wished she'd had the chance to be. Forty-two and acting like a schoolgirl who'd never been kissed. It was such silliness yet such dizzy pretence. And Alan opening doors and kissing her hand, for goodness sake. She shouldn't have been shocked at the proposal, when it came. Alan was a man and even the sweetest of men won't wait forever. She'd just hoped to play the game a little longer. Of course, she said yes, and then she wept, and Alan thought it was happiness. She let him believe it; how could she ever have explained her grief?

He'd been so wonderful with the grandkids, little Angie and Mel scampering in the backyard when Donna came to visit. Or on Saturday nights when they babysat, Alan dandling the girls on his knee. He always had lollies for them, and they ran straight to him. She was sure it was completely innocent back then, whatever Donna now believed. Of Sylvie's three daughters, Donna had always been the one closest to her mother. The others had moved far away, to the Gold Coast and Sydney, but Donna married and settled in Altona, barely ten minutes up the road, and Angie was born the same year that Sylvie married Alan.

It was deeply hurtful to Sylvie that Donna didn't call her anymore. She used to ring every Tuesday and Friday night, without fail, and now the silence on those days was an unending reproach. But why should she be punished for what they were saying Alan had done to the girls?

You knew something, Donna said. Or you should have known, you would have if you'd wanted to. When she was fourteen Angie kept a knife under her pillow when she stayed over, she was so scared of Alan. How can you support that man after what he did to your own grandchildren? That man. He'd become that man.

But how could she have known? Those nights when Alan used to drink his VBs on the veranda, the insects zapping against the violet coil over the door, when he'd call for Angie to come keep him company: 'Angel' he called her, had since she was a baby. C'mon Angel, be nice to your poor old gramps. Now they were saying that was when it had happened. When he touched her. Well all Sylvie could say was, she'd never seen anything. Could it have been so bad? So terrible that Angie had to sleep with a knife? Sylvie had been in and out and seen them together, and Angie was laughing as he bounced her up and down, that was the game they played.

Maybe it was all her fault, she thought on restless nights alone in the empty marriage bed. She hadn't been the perfect wife and who could blame Alan if he looked elsewhere? Of course it should never have been a five-year-old girl; that was wrong, there was no excuse. But perhaps if she'd been better able to please him, none of this would have happened. She knew he was disappointed in her, but she had never understood what made other women so keen on sex. Secretly she suspected they were putting it on. It was men who wanted it, men who insisted on it, men who were liable to become dangerous if they didn't get it. Sex belonged to them, not to women, not to girls. It certainly didn't belong to Sylvie.

She looked at her hand, folded in Alan's stronger, bigger one. An old woman's hand, just bones and blue veins under skin gone too soft, like the belly of a grass-rotted peach. What right did they have to put her through this at her age? Both their hands were inert, awkward, Alan all at sea with her now that his familiar manly postures were all shattered. Still he wore the fragments, grasping the chances he had to tell her what to do, to puff up his collapsed chest. She caught herself telling him tales of her ineptitude to save herself from the naked confusion and strain she saw in his gaze. These stories had become part of their routine, something they relied on in order to know their roles. She should never have sprayed the wasps herself, he told her. That was a professional job, for people who knew what they were doing.

Something came in the post, she told him. Some papers. I don't know who sent them.

What are they?

I'm not sure ... I think they might be the ... victim statement.

Alan's eyes widened.

Who sent them to you? Which one?

I told you, Alan, I don't know. Kay's, I think. I saw her name—Alan's hand jerked out of hers.

You haven't read it ...

No. No ... No. I couldn't.

His shoulders relaxed slightly.

You're going to get rid of it, aren't you, he said—a command not a question. You should throw it out, Sylvie. You know what she's like. I bet she was the one behind it too, the bitch. It's not enough I'm in here, she wants to turn you against me too. Fuck!

She hated hearing him swear. He never used to before, leastways not when she was around, not in front of a lady. He always looked down on that sort of thing.

I don't know, Alan. Jan says I should read it ...

Jan? Your counsellor? Why? It's all lies, Sylvie. Anyone could see that. Kay's a drug addict. She said so herself in court. I can't understand how anyone believed that pack of lies.

Jan thinks—

Jan thinks! What about me? What about what I think? Your husband? Bloody do-gooders!

She recoiled at his outburst. She knew he hated the welfare workers who were now a part of Sylvie's life. And his: where would he be without the Salvos, the family liaison workers, the guy who handled the canteen money Sylvie put in for him each week? Yet he hated all of them, for interfering in his life, for reminding him of his helplessness. There was nothing he could do for himself anymore. And she could see how it had diminished him.

But Sylvie had come to depend on her sessions with Jan. Sometimes it was the only conversation she had in the entire fortnight, apart from phone calls and visits with Alan, which weren't the same. Alan wanted a report on everything she did, but only in order to exercise some kind of remote control over her. Sometimes she thought Jan was the only person who had ever really listened to her. And Jan thought she should read the statement, whoever had sent it. There were things that needed facing, she said. She even wanted Sylvie to talk about her past, something Sylvie was determined to put off for as long as she could, even forever. The past was past, the past was over. And if it was gone, if you couldn't find it anywhere, who was to say it was real at all?

Kay was the reason why Alan had got ten years—a 'brick' in the prison lingo Sylvie was becoming familiar with in spite of herself. Alan had admitted to Sylvie that he might have touched Angie the wrong way. According to him it was through her clothes and only happened once or twice, when he'd drunk a few too many tinnies, but even so, he should have known better. But the things Kay had said in court—terrible things that Sylvie had blocked from her mind: Alan would have to have been an animal. It was impossible to believe any of it. Alan said there were women who were like that, women with a chip on their shoulder who would make up a rape allegation just to kick a man when he was down. If what she was saying was true, why hadn't she made the allegation earlier, before the thing with Angie came up?

And yet ... It troubled her.

But why? she asked Alan, as she had done before. Why would she make up such awful things? After we were so nice to her, taking her away camping with us when her mum was in hospital and her dad needed a break. And such a ... complicated lie.

But the question only made Alan angrier. How the hell should he know how a drug addict thinks? Maybe she actually believes it herself. People can do that, you know. End up believing their own lies. His eyes challenging and baleful and hurt so that Sylvie felt sorry and backed down.

After this the visit was ruined, though to tell the truth there was nothing much to ruin, what with the strip search and Alan getting so anxious and uncomfortable about the victim statement. Sylvie had started feeling unwell. Her sciatica was playing up again and quite frankly she was feeling a little nauseous. The antiseptic was cloying in her throat and she wondered if she mightn't be allergic to it. Alan started talking about the wasps again, telling her she should get an exterminator in, just to make sure, Mortein wasn't meant for that kind of job, you need a proper fumigation and on and on so she stopped listening. The wasps were dead, and she'd done it herself, and why didn't he just admit that that was what he didn't like, seeing her learning to do things for herself?

Stepping out into the cold air on Spencer Street she felt momentarily disoriented, everything sharp-etched and bright, a slap of reality and winter. She crossed the road to the tram stop stiffly, her back protesting after the plastic chair she'd been sitting in for an hour.

It might have been the old man eating the banana at the back of the tram that made her think of it, of the nine-year-old girl running down the street on an errand for her mother, for an egg or a lemon or what-have-you from Mrs Barker.

It was hard to say now for sure, but she thought she remembered a happy girl. She was pretty sure she remembered it all the way it was, the squat orange houses with their lawns yellowing in the late summer dry. And jumping to pluck the hard little prunus plums from the trees on the nature strip; she liked them sour. Mrs Barker had rosemary growing along her wire fence. Sylvie had picked sprigs from it before, on Sundays for lamb roast. She knocked on the door and stood hopping on the step, bored within twenty seconds when nobody answered and ready to run back for another plum. But then the door swung open and it was Mr Barker standing there in his singlet behind the wire mesh.

Sylvia, he said.

She asked if Mrs Barker was there but he said no, she was out.

Oh, said Sylvie, unsure now what to do. She'd never asked a man for anything before, and she didn't much care for Mr. Barker. He had a funny smell.

It's okay, she said, and went to turn for the gate, but Mr Barker opened the flywire door.

It was very hot, he said. Surely she would like a drink before she went home? Or a banana. Did she like bananas? And he did a gnashing thing with his teeth, in some sort of stupid imitation of a tiger.

At home it was quiet, and of course everything was just as she left it, the opened envelope with the victim impact statement still lying on the kitchen table. She heard Alan's anxious voice in her head: *You're going to get rid of it, aren't you.* Sylvie made herself a cup of tea to wash the aftertaste of antiseptic from her mouth. She normally liked to drink her tea weak, but this time it didn't do the trick, so she made herself a second one, a strong one, and it felt good, it felt different. It was almost dark in the kitchen by the time she finished the second cup so she turned on the light. And then she put on her reading glasses.

White Summer

James woke in pitch darkness and with a lurch of terror found that he did not know who or where he was. He sprang from the bed, hitting his head hard on something overhead. Light and pain flashed and he started to cry out, not 'Help! Help!' but 'Hilfe! Hilfe!' Why was he speaking German? A moment later the light switched on and Anja was standing in the doorway in a dressing-gown.

'James, was ist los?' *What's the matter?*

He heard Karl, Anja's eight-year-old son, cry out. He had woken the whole house with his stupid yelling. He wanted to explain himself, but when he reached for the German, it wasn't there. He stared at her, his mouth opening and closing like a fish's. Finally he mumbled, 'Es tut mir Leid,' *I'm sorry*, and sat back down on the bed. Anja said something he didn't follow, then hit the light switch, plunging him back into darkness. Karl's wailing went on—*Mutti, Mutti*—like an echo of his own cry, and he heard Anja's footsteps in the corridor as she went to comfort him.

His room was in a garret at the top of the house; he had hit his head on the ceiling where it sloped sharply over his bed. In the mornings he would open the blinds and look out on a landscape that could hardly have been more remote from Sydney's dry brilliance. Fat steeple-roofed houses clustered on the damp plain of the Ruhr-Gebiet under a low gunmetal sky. As days passed, erratic icy flurries gave way to a thick silent downpour that buried everything. For a time, before the whiteness wore out the eye, the pristine dunes of snow accomplished a miracle, transforming that prosaic scene into a fairy-tale tableau.

The cold had taken him by surprise; it was beyond anything he had encountered before, knifing straight through his warmest clothes. Even in the centrally heated house of his hosts, he felt persecuted by a constant chill. They believed that an overheated house hampered adjustment to the cold outside. He learned a German word that encapsulated his experience: *trostlos*. Comfortless, hopeless—there is no perfect translation, but James understood the word exactly. It described an abject condition in which there is no respite from misery.

Anja's husband Dieter worked for a major pharmaceutical company. He was a big, thick-fingered man, almost the stereotype of the German executive, fattened on Bratwurst and Kartoffeln. One evening he knocked on the door of James's room. He stood in the small space looking flustered, his big hands fidgeting.

'I just vanted to … I vondered how are you going?' he said, using English for the first time since James had arrived. They had told him he would learn better if he were allowed to converse in German only.

James forced a smile. 'Fine. Thank you.'

Dieter sweated. 'Vee are vorried for you. You don't seem … heppy.' He blushed, apparently embarrassed by the word. 'Did you, did you vant to… talk?' His pained expression gave the impression he had fish-bones caught his throat. It was obvious he had been put up to this by his wife.

'No, no. I'm just … I'm just cold.'

'Oh, cold!' Dieter's face beamed with relief. He had safely crossed the tightrope to secure ground. 'Ja. It is cold this year. But in Shermany vee heff a saying: Who freezes is either poor or stupid.' He laughed and gave James's arm a hearty thump. 'Vell, let me know if …' He petered out. 'Gute Nacht,' he said, and retreated.

There had been a day not long before he had left Australia when everything had fallen in on him. Glen Thomas cornered him in the school toilet. 'Poofta,' he sneered—his usual taunt—then put him in a head lock and banged his head against the stinking metal of the urinal. 'Want a lolly?' he said, forcing James's face down towards the foul yellow blobs of soap in the piss-clogged gutter. For an awful moment he thought he was going to be forced to eat one, but then as suddenly as it had begun, the attack was over. Glen released his neck from the vice of his arm, then stood indifferently at the urinal, pissing on the spot where he'd held James's head a moment before. Still in shock, James continued to stand there, until Glen said, 'You checking out my dick? You really are a poofter, aren't you?'

On the way home, Glen and two of his cronies were lounging against a wall, smoking and taking to turns to spit on the footpath. James tried to ignore them, to look resolutely ahead, but as he passed, they made a sudden move towards him and he ran. He heard them laugh. It was too hot for them to bother with a chase.

'Run, faggot, run,' he heard one of them say.

Later that night, he ate dinner with his family. That was still in the time when nothing was said, when truths could not be named, but hung in the air, oppressive like the heat before the change. The time of silence and lies. His parents were still together, bonded by nothing more than the thin glue of routine, pretence and fear of change. When the ice-cream came for dessert, and James put the first spoonful into his mouth, he felt suddenly like a five-year-old child, and an awful sadness arose in him. He began to cry silently, tears sliding down and mixing saltily with the ice-cream he continued to spoon into his mouth. Everyone kept eating, and all that could be heard was the clinking of spoons on bowls and the suffocating sound of silence.

Later, he went out into the garden, and in a sudden rage, kicked all the heads off the cabbages. Then he kicked the heads until they were all smashed and broken, debris all over the garden. But the aggression brought him no relief. There was pain in everything his mind touched.

The garden had fallen into darkness and through the kitchen window he could see his parents washing up, his brother making a cup of tea. It was an unreal pantomime, and standing among the ruined cabbages, he felt as removed from the domestic normality of the scene as if he were watching a film of events a century in the past. He went to his room and fell on his bed, pain swarming over him like a cloud of bees. He bit down hard on his anguish—nobody must hear him—and the thought *I don't want to go* screamed in his head. But the ticket was booked, the arrangements made, there was no getting out of it.

Anja brought him an aerogramme from his mother telling him that the summer had turned into a stinker. Three days over forty in a row. But here the nights fell to minus twenty. Along the road, the cars were stacked with snow like wedding cakes. James helped the family cover a pine tree in the backyard with tinsel and baubles, and Karl danced around it, the magic of the snow merging in his mind with the enchantment of Christmas. But in spite of the familiar images of snow and Christmas trees, to James it seemed that summer had been abducted and buried beneath an arctic freeze. A white summer. He stood in his garret window, watching darkness fall at four o'clock, the twinkle of Christmas lights emerging everywhere, as if to replace the stars that remained hidden behind the permanent bank of cloud. To die of cold, he recalled, was supposed to be blissful, after a certain point. An overdose of snow like heroin, death in a beautiful dream opiated by cold.

He was sitting in the living room studying the list of German vocab he'd made for the day, when he looked up to find a girl, a young woman standing there. Under a crazy mass of black curls, her eyes regarded him with a warmth that startled him. It was a gaze that seemed to see through him, to laugh off his shame and self-doubt as if with a brush of her hand she could wipe it away like frost on a window. He stood, confused, and she came forward and reached out her hand. 'Hallo,' she said. 'Ich bin Emilie. Ich bin hier als *au pair.*' He heard how the language was awkward to her, the way her French accent tried to soften it. Her handshake barely registered in his mind at the time, but years later he would realise he could still recall the sensation of it exactly, the warmth and inexplicable affection of it.

She was from Boulogne. She played the piano. Her German was bad—worse than James's—her English just a little better, so they conversed in a mix of the two languages, cutting out the English when their hosts were around. Her room was in the basement, next to the laundry where she did the family's washing and ironing. There was also a games room there with a pool table, a computer for Karl to play games on. They sat down there and played Uno, laughing at their linguistic mix-ups, at the strangeness of Germans, at everything. She laughed at the way he laughed.

'You 'ave a funny laugh,' she laughed.

'Nein.'

'Ja. You do.'

'Was ist so komisch?'

'I don't know. You sound like this.' She made an absurd whinnying sound.

'No, I don't. I don't sound anything like that,' he laughed.

'There. You are doing it again.' She made the noise again.

'Hör auf! Du klingst wie ein Pferd.' Laughter was making his sides hurt, his head dizzy.

'It is you who sound like a 'orse.'

The laughter, her intoxicating proximity, made him suddenly brave. 'Do you have a boyfriend … in France?'

'Nein.'

'Are we in English or German?'

And they both laughed till they sobbed.

They were woken one morning while it was still dark to go hunting in the Schwarzwald. Standing in the gloom of the garage Emilie looked as pale and dazed as he felt. The Mercedes sped along the autobahn, 180 ks in the icy fog, rapid-fire German on the radio reporting news he couldn't follow. The window was cold on his forehead as he watched the factories loom out of the grey. Behind concrete sound-barriers, the hills were piled with the small, drab houses of the factory workers, hunkered down against the bitter weather. Then frozen fields and distant farmhouses half lost in the blur, lives he couldn't imagine.

The warmth of the car's heater, the engine's steady hum lulled him. He dozed off, and for a time he was somewhere he belonged, some formless comforting place at the borders of nothingness. Then the engine noise cut out like a blanket pulled away to expose the hard silence beneath. He woke. Anja turned in the passenger seat. She smiled at him, a maternal smile he was familiar with. It told him she saw an unhappy child in him, she responded to a lost boy. But he was seventeen; childhood was locked and barred behind him now. In any case he did not love this stranger; he would not let her mother him. He looked away without returning the smile. Outside, in the drifting fog and snow, a fat man was gathering shotguns from the boot of his BMW.

When he opened the car door, the cold hit him in the face, twined around his throat. He stood stamping the icy slush underfoot, clamping his hands in the warmth of his armpits. Dieter checked the barrel of his shotgun, sighted it at the sky that seemed to be collapsing onto their shoulders. Anja came over and gave James a slim metal box like a cigarette case. It was warm to the touch. She opened it to show him a coal smouldering inside in a woolly insulated bed. To keep his hands warm, she explained, pressing it into his coat pocket in that motherly way.

Of course, they didn't give him a gun. Instead he and Emilie joined the line of beaters who marched through the forest bashing the undergrowth with sticks to drive out the game. His feet went numb and the snow melted on his collar and trickled down his neck.

After a time the trees cleared and gave way to a field of dense scrub. Away from the shelter of the trees, the wind was sharp and bitter, snaking into his collar however tight he drew it. As they traversed the field, a small covey of grouse burst from the bushes. The hunters stood and fired. Stinging pellets of shot spat down onto James's upturned face, and he covered his head with his arms, almost crying out. One by one the birds fell, plummeted dead or dying out of the air. Only one kept rising for a time, defying the guns, heaving its body higher until it began to fade into the fog. And then finally, a puff of feathers and it, too, spiralled down. Dogs bounded forward to collect the kill.

With the limp, bloody grouse slung over their shoulders, the hunters were flushed with excitement and manly bonhomie. They slapped one another's backs and joked as they crossed the field and once again entered the silence of the Black Forest. The beaters spread out through the trees, growing further apart until it became hard to keep track of the line. He could see Emilie moving far to his right, every now and again striking at the scrub in a desultory fashion. In the near-solitude, the beating felt meaningless and James let his arm drop and trudged on in silence. The silver case in his pocket kept the fingers of one hand warm while the rest of him shivered.

He heard a shout behind him. A man with a gun came running through the trees towards him. 'Was ist los mit dir?' he shouted. 'Warum treibst du nicht? Schlag doch!' It was the man he'd seen earlier taking his guns out of the BMW. His face was red, his jowls quivering. James could only make out half of what he was shouting at him. But he understood that he was being told to beat and half-heartedly whacked the bushes. To his amazement, there was a rustle and a startled hare bolted out of the undergrowth. A cry went up, blurts of excited German, as it shot terrified across the line of beaters. It jinked fast through the trees while the guns banged and the fat men shouted. *Go*, he thought.

The man raised his barrel. His eyes contracted to murderous points as he tracked the path of the dodging hare. The blast crashed against James's nerves, but the hare was still going.

'Scheisse,' the man swore, but he didn't lower his gun. There was a second barrel. The hare cut across a clearing towards the safety of a dense thicket. The man swung the gun to take aim, but now James was in his line of fire. He was staring into the shotgun's smoking muzzle.

'Aus dem Weg!' the man barked. But James didn't move. He stared back into the black hole of the gun, of the hunter's eyes. He had never thought of himself as having much in the way of courage, but somehow he found the ability to stand where he was, to paralyse himself, to stretch out the moment of defiance one second longer, one second longer. He saw ice in the hunter's moustache, the escalating rage on his face, watched as the thought of pulling the trigger, the easiness of it, the release of it, passed over the man's face. And then the barrel dropped.

'Du Idiot,' the man ranted, apoplectic. 'Bist du total blöd? Ich hätte dich erschießen können.' *I could have shot you.*

James looked down, letting the abuse wash over him. Snow had melted in his boots and his feet were freezing.

In the late afternoon the whole hunting expedition drove to a vast mansion owned by one of the hunters, a work colleague of Dieter's and a senior executive in the company. One room was decked out in mediaeval fashion, mounted stags' heads on the walls, and here they laid out their kill on a rough-hewn wooden table. The grouse, a couple of hares, and their prize quarry, a small doe. Its head lolled from the edge of the table, eyes dull, and a crimson slime trickled from its mouth to gloss the slate floor.

They threw logs into a huge fireplace, drank beer from enormous pewter steins, lit up pipes and cigars. The centuries seemed to vanish like a vapour. James sat on a bench in the corner, watching the spectacle of modern executives atavistically transformed into barbarians, Vikings roaring after the slaughter. And there was something intoxicating about it all: blood, beer, the heat of alcohol and fire after the snowy forest.

'I think they 'ave gone crazy.'

Emilie had slipped onto the bench beside him.

'Wahnsinn,' agreed James.

They sat a moment contemplating the scene. Then she seized his hand, pulled him to his feet. 'Let's go.'

He followed her through a door into a long, silent corridor. 'We shouldn't be here,' he said. She kept hold of his hand and pulled him along the corridor.

'Look at this.' She gestured through an open door and, to James's amazement, he saw there was a huge indoor swimming pool there. On the far side of the darkened room he could make out the pine doors of what he assumed was a sauna. Through another door they saw a small cinema, then another room set up as a disco. Other enormous rooms stood empty, as if the owners' imaginations had simply fallen short of their wealth. The money was beyond James's comprehension.

At the end of the corridor a door opened onto a snowy courtyard, lit by floodlights. It was silent apart from the muffled sound of discordant, raucous singing from the hunters at the other end of the house. Flakes fell and eddied like particles of light over the unbroken blanket of white. Where the lights ended the night was a perfect void, unfathomable as a pupil. In its darkness, the wind moved, stirring over the frozen forests of Germany. Emilie ran laughing out onto the pristine snow, her feet punching through it, leaving holes of blue shadow. She turned around, surrounded by a pale halo of iridescence cast by the lights in the icy air. She crouched to gather the snow in her hands and James, seeing what she was doing, ran forward and caught her around the waist, the snowball disintegrating over his back as she tried to throw it. He pinned her down on the snow. Her face was close, her breath a warm cloud on his cheeks. 'Du warst mutig heute,' she said. *You were brave today.* And then they were kissing, her nose cold against his face, but her mouth hot and tasting of the mysteries of her body.

It was not a long kiss, by the standards of other kisses he would one day know. But it was long enough for her to take his cold hand inside her clothes, like a bird she was saving, taking home folded into her breast. Long enough for his hand to feel her heart beating in the soft, warm valley there, for his fingers to grow warm and spread over the swell of her, to feel her nipple rise under his palm.

Fifteen years later, he would wake in his bed in Sydney, with the same panicked moment of amnesia he had once known in Germany, and when the disorientation cleared, the knowledge struck his heart as if it had been a brass bell: *I am not at home.* But this place was his home. There was nowhere else to go back to. His mind floundered for a moment seeking that emotional reference point and then, to his astonishment, it was Emilie's face he saw rising out of the obscurity of memory. For a while he lay on his back, tears making hot tracks to his ears, then sleep drifted over. And in the morning when he woke the memory was gone, the summer birds were singing, and he rolled over into his wife's sleepy embrace.

Comrade Vasilii Goes to War

Strike a match out here at night and it's the only light in a hundred kilometres at least. That's if you don't count the stars, which is a good idea, because if you did, your head would start to spin before you got to ten. You'd drown in stars out here if you were tall enough. Our generator died four months ago and we've been without lights or heating ever since. We thank God it's summer and pray that Captain Sviatoslavich comes good on his promise to send out a repairman before the snow starts to fall. But frankly we don't hold out much hope. We never believe a word he tells us.

There's about fifty metres between our outpost and theirs, just a bare patch of dust. No barbed wire or boom gates mark the border. To tell the truth, we've no idea where it is. Sometimes, when we're particularly bored, we play this stupid game, drawing a line through the dust with our rifle butts and taunting each other—step over that line, Comrade, and you're a dead man! This here is Uzekhstan! And Vasilii—he's the one that started this shit—he'll step right over and draw another line ten metres further back and declare that that is the true border, and that we are in fact invaders on the sovereign territory of Ozakhstan! And so it goes, until we get bored with it all and decide to go inside and get pissed on Vasilii's vodka.

To avoid confusion, I should point out that I too am Vasilii. Well, it's a common name. Not that he is anything like me. He is intelligent, handsome and tall and reads Tolstoy and Dostoyevsky. He even reads some English writer called Shakespeare. When he's drunk enough he stands in front of the window looking as tall and desperate as Rasputin and booms out sad English words that make all our hairs stand up, even though we don't understand a bit of it. I, on the other hand, am stupid, ugly and short, and the only things I read are letters from Raisa, the girl who, for reasons I cannot justify, loves me. I've been reading the same letters for months, because that's how often the mail truck bothers to come by.

Vlad isn't a much better specimen. He's fat as a pig and has flat feet that stink, so I never let him take his boots off, even at night. Every now and then I tell him to wash them, and then I cross the border to play poker with Vasilii and Anton so I don't have to be there when he does. Actually I shouldn't order poor Vlad around like that. Technically he's my superior officer, but even though I am stupid, he is really stupider. Vlad has no Raisa, or any other girl. He reads letters from his mama and cries. He is such a baby.

We got sent out here to the border because we were the very worst soldiers in the academy. We weren't cut out to be soldiers, but everyone has to be a soldier in Uzekhstan. Vlad should have been a pig farmer or a panel beater. As for me, I wouldn't have minded working in a bar selling beer to western girls in tank tops and short denim skirts who want to ficky-fick with an Uzekhstani boy. Sorry, Raisa! I am having dirty thoughts again. It's this cold, lonely steppe. After a while it starts to turn a man into a wolf.

Captain Sviatoslavich told us the situation was this: we don't want their bastards coming over here, and your job is to stop them if they try. This was stupid. Ozakhstan is exactly the same as Uzekhstan. Everybody knows this. Escaping from one to the other is like slapping your left cheek because you're tired of slapping your right. But because we built a border post, they had to build one too. To stop our bastards going over there. Which is Vasilii and Anton's job.

I don't know about Anton, but I don't think they sent Vasilii out here for being a bad soldier. It is obvious to everyone he should probably be a general and lead the whole Ozakhstan army. I think he was sent here for being overheard calling the Ozakhstan president a vodka-pickled, nepotistic, barnyard-animal-fucking, corrupt licker of fat western arses. When a nice secret policeman visited him to ask him about this indiscretion, Vasilii swore he was referring to the president of Uzekhstan (which is incidentally quite plausible) but a week later they sent him here anyway.

When they first arrived, we were such prigs. Refusing to say good morning when we happened to be out having a piss at the same time, spitting at the Ozakhstan flag and all that nonsense. But Vasilii wore us down with his charm and his stupid pranks. He was forever wandering around in the abandoned space between the outposts smoking a cigarette and gazing into the sky like he was working out some problem of astronomical measurement. It drove me crazy that he acted like there was no border there at all, so one day I went out and drew a line in the dirt and told him never to cross it. You can guess what he did. It made me laugh, but I was too angry to show it so I turned my back on him. And then I heard his voice purring right behind my shoulder. *Are you laughing comrade?* That was how he won.

Sometimes I think he only did it to supplement his miserable wages by luring us into those dreadful all-night poker games. I don't know how he does it, but it always goes the same. Every time I pick up my cards and there's a sweet row of queens or something, he folds. In the end you get so sick of it you bluff him, and he pushes you all the way over the edge and rakes in the pot with a pair of tens or something. Vlad gets so furious his face goes purple and he throws his cards and storms out. Then five minutes later, he'll stick his big sheepish head back in and beg to be let into the game again. Vasilii is always willing to forgive him.

This morning our radio suddenly blared. It was Captain Sviatoslavich. The crisis has escalated! he shouted at us.

What crisis would that be, Captain Shitoslavich? I asked, winking at Vlad.

The political crisis, you idiot! screamed the captain. We are at war with Ozakhstan!

Vlad and I looked at one another, our mouths gaping dumbly. You must engage the enemy!

I breathed a sigh of relief. We were off the hook. I'd thought for a moment we were getting a recall. But for once Vlad was actually smarter than me. What do you mean by 'engage the enemy', sir? he asked.

What do you think I mean, you lard-arsed dolt? Shoot them! Now! Over and out.

Then I understood, and the dawning realisation of our situation hit me like a fist to the guts. I went to the window and looked out over the dusty no-man's-land of the border. I could see Vasilii and Anton playing cards as usual. Obviously, they didn't know we were at war yet, but it would only be a matter of time. We had to act swiftly.

I threw Vlad his gun, which he held at arm's length like it was a poisonous snake. I could see he was about to cry so I knew I had to take control. Why they promoted him above me I will never understand. We're not going to shoot them, alright? I said. We're just going to take them prisoner. I looked him in the eye. Okay? He nodded, wide-eyed like a child.

It was only fifty metres from one door to the other, but that lugubrious march seemed longer than any of the exhausting forced marches from our academy days.

When we stepped into the room, Vasilii looked up from his card game and gave me his easy handsome grin. So Vasilii, have you come to shoot me now? he asked, raising an eyebrow.

In such stupid situations as this, it is impossible to be a real human being, so you read from a script, like a moron robot.

Comrade Vasilii, I am taking you prisoner of the state of Uzekhstan, I said, pointing the barrel at his chest. Vasilii's smile stayed on his face, but I saw his eyes change as the reality of the situation dawned on him. He looked cool as my grandmother's cucumbers, but a drop of sweat ran down his brow and into one of his eyes.

He stood up slowly, and as I stood there shaking, he unholstered his pistol and pointed it straight at my heart.

Comrade Vasilii, he said, I am taking you prisoner of the state of Ozakhstan. I don't know if he thought this was funny. He might have been smiling about anything.

Anton was now pointing his gun at Vlad, and Vlad was pointing his gun at Anton.

Things were getting over my head, so I turned to my superior officer. What do we do now? I asked.

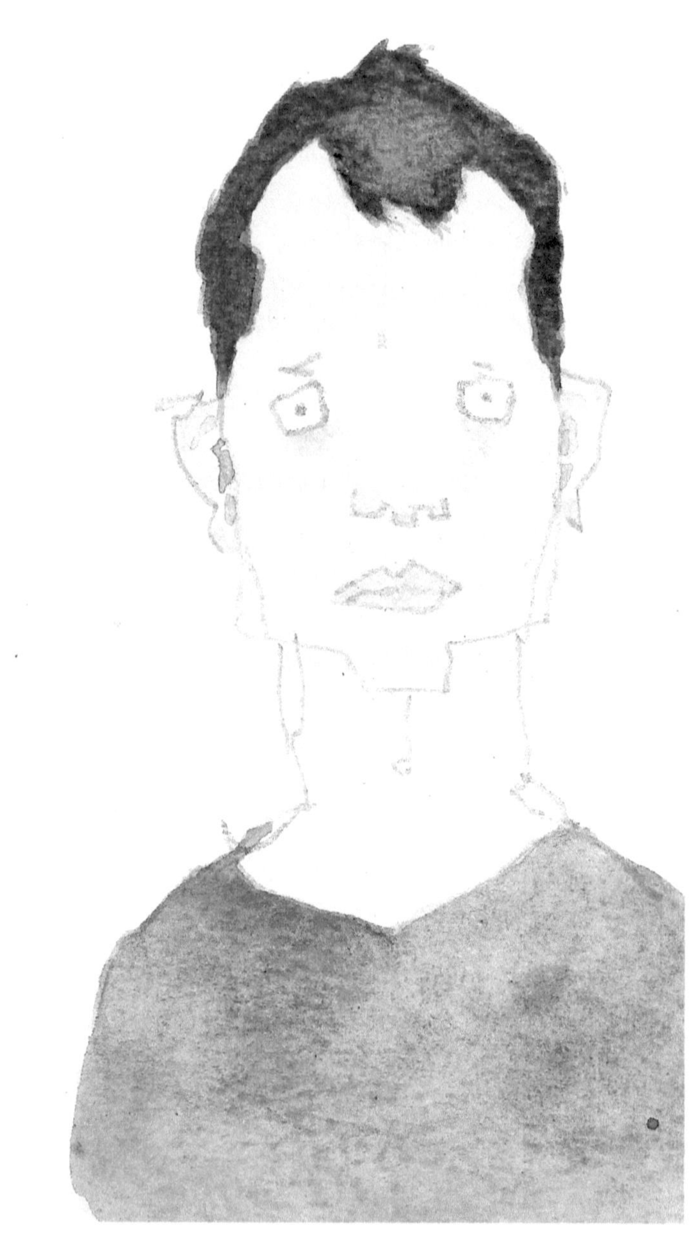

This Old Man

My son is singing in the back seat as the car winds along the road between Cairns and Port Douglas. Every turn along the crumpled boundary of sea and land reveals something I have not seen before, the blank map in my mind flooding with colour and detail. Ben's happy, I know. I can hear it in his voice: adventure and safety together in the warm sea wind blowing in his face through the half-open window.

This old man

He played ... zero!

He played knickknack on my ... hero!

Dad, he calls out.

Yes, Ben.

He played knickknack on my hero!

Yes, Ben.

Is that funny, Dad?

Umm ... not unless you're six years old.

Why not?

Well, once you got to zero—I shrug—he was either going to be playing knickknack on your hero, or on Robert De Niro.

Blessed silence for a time. There are smudges of smoke from the cane fires, and coconut palms and macadamias, and waves nibbling the black rocky shore, and great fibrous fruit in the trees, but the sky is a featureless grey glare. Here and there a wan stain of blue. My eyes blur, my back aches. It's been a long drive.

This old man

He played five ...

Ben?

Yes, Dad?

Can you stop singing that song for a bit, please?

Okay, Dad.

Then he sees something: Look!

He's pointing in the direction of the sea, but I see nothing except the hard, flat light from the water.

What?

Look! Look!

He's about jumping out of his seatbelt.

I can't, Ben, I'm driving!

Oh you missed it! He's furious now, his seraphic face instantly souring to something far less pleasant.

I'm sorry, Ben. I'm trying to drive. What was it?

A tree, Dad! It was an amazing tree. Can we go back?

I get cunning. I've learned to negotiate the shape of his mind, the catching points of his personality, as one steps around furniture at home in the dark.

Oh, the tree! Yes, I saw that! It was amazing, wasn't it?

For a moment in the rear-view mirror I see him struggle to change emotional direction. Then the shadow passes from his face. Happiness is restored now he's shared his wonder. He leans into that slice of wind that's coming in through the window, his blue eyes flickering in the gusts, and his hair dancing free. Rapturous and forgetful, he starts to sing:

This old man ...

The moment when I learned of Ben's existence is preserved in my memory with the miraculous detail of a fossil in amber. Maddy had just stepped through the front door. She was wearing a white angora jumper, the summer light that spilled down the hall making a fine soft haze around the fertile swell of her breasts. The sweet smell of wattle pollen followed her, the hum of bees and lawnmowers. She brushed past me. I'm pregnant. Even though we'd only been together for six months, three living together, even though she would never have planned it, I could tell she was happy. She kept moving, her back to me so I wouldn't see the excitement just beneath the adult grimness she was officially wearing for the occasion. I made an ineffectual gesture with my open palms. I'd been knocked out of gear and my thoughts and emotions spun without engaging. I was empty of anything real, anything remotely adequate. A smile arose to take possession of my features, the involuntary smile that the immature sometimes wear on hearing of a death.

It wasn't real: the news, the smile, anything. I instinctively knew there had to be a way out. Other than the obvious. There seemed to be a certain obscenity lurking in the word abortion, which the now preferred term termination only went part way towards eradicating. If abortion was awful, blood-stained by right-to-life images of foetuses dismembered with boning scissors, termination had a sinister, newspeak ring to it. Didn't the mafia, the CIA terminate? There had to be some other way, some escape clause between the binary alternatives, between black and white, yes and no. There always had been before.

Some time in the coming days, as the uncompromising nature of the situation began to dawn on me, I arrived at a position. I gallantly declared: Whatever you decide, I'll support you. A politician's line, of course, fooling nobody. Whatever you decide. A masterstroke of abnegation. I hated this new found emptiness that seemed to speak for me, this puppetry of understanding: nods caresses murmurs. I searched for the man, the father, but finding him absent jerked and muttered and marionetted my way through visits to clinics and counsellors. We started taking phone calls in the other room. We closed the door.

I'm carrying heavy suitcases up the stairs to our room at the resort, while Ben lugs his own little bag. At the top of the first flight of concrete stairs I stop to rest a moment. Ben is thrilled to spot a translucent gecko inhabiting the concrete seam between the wall and the ceiling of the corridor, a ghostly comic creature. The stairwell is open to the air at the back, allowing a view of tropical foliage, tangled liana and fat heavy leaves trailing spider webs.

Look, Dad, says Ben.

Yes, I say, once again uncertain what I should be seeing.

It looks exciting, doesn't it?

It sure does, I say, and pick up the suitcases again to tackle the second flight of steps.

When I paid for it in Melbourne, I had imagined luxury, but the room is disappointing: a functional, anonymous 'unit' with a sliding door onto a tiny balcony that overlooks the swimming pool. In the overcast glare of the afternoon, some kids are playing pool volleyball. I stand there awhile watching them as Ben plays with the little packets of soap deposited on the ends of the beds. Pretty girls with small, new breasts, a fat pasty kid and a taller, good-looking one whose every lunge for the ball is alpha-male choreography. The girls giggle and tease and retreat, reserving the right to exploit the ambiguity that suspends the game between child's play and courtship ritual. Not far away the thirtysomethings are arranged like shish kebabs on the plastic deckchairs, creased brown flesh exposed for the benefit of whatever UV makes it through the cloud. A bull-shouldered man in tiny Speedos drinks on an underwater stool beside the pool bar, his pale eyes sliding and swivelling over his gin as the women go by.

Later, we go into town for the first time, looking for something to eat. I hold Ben's hand to cross the sandy streets of the tourist precinct, restaurant touts hail me, and even though I am hungry, the garish shops, the steel chairs of the restaurant forecourts repel me and soon we have reached the place where the street meets the beach, boats jostling in the marina and twilight falling over the palm trees, but nowhere to eat. We have to backtrack. Ben is hungry and getting difficult, dragging his feet, so it's eenie-meenie-minie-mo and whatever restaurant; we order pizzas and Ben colours in a pirate picture with crayons that the harried waitress brings—they're a family-friendly restaurant.

But we're not a family, objects Ben, who has recently discovered the joys of pedantry.

Yes, we are.

But Mum isn't here.

Two people can be a family.

No, they can't.

Look here's your pizza.

There's a woman eating alone across the way, her table an island of concentration and composure amid the hubbub. Middle-aged, I think. Then: no, my age. The candle in front of her flickers in a subdued way, shimmering through the chardonnay she sips between carefully excised nibbles. She is not a family; I'm prepared to concede that.

We're going to have fun. I take Ben up to Kuranda on the cable car, wobbling high over the treetops. Ulysses butterflies floating like little shreds of sky or flying fish between the swells of rainforest. At Kuranda we eat hot dogs and Golden Gaytimes for lunch, what the hell we're on holiday, and Ben's face is a mess of melted chocolate bits and tomato sauce. The heat saps us. He needs to go the toilet. Now. We have to run in the end, and some leaks out, wetting his trousers. He's ashamed and won't leave the toilet block even though the train is coming in ten minutes to take us back down the mountain. It wrenches to command him in his wretched condition, but what choice do I have?

He doesn't know it, but I am six years old too, feeling every miserable half-choked sob as he goes through the crowd, head hung, not knowing that nobody notices or cares about his little accident. On the train he presses his grubby, tear-streaked face to the window, so the rowdy boy next to him won't see his eyes, and I know not to hug him. Some burdens I cannot share. Then he loses himself in the passing gorges and waterfalls and suddenly he's pointing out a coloured bird to me, the smile on his face like sun breaking through a wet day.

When I was six my father and I turned over rocks in tidal pools near Anglesea, and discovered many miracles that seem to have disappeared over the years. Perhaps it was the effect of people like us, reckless wonderers, even though we always put the rocks back the way they were. I once found a mysterious crimson brain on the rocks, some protean creature like raspberry aeroplane jelly spilled from its mould before it was fully set. I took it home in a jar, and it died, whatever it was. It stank in unexpected and incredible ways and completely liquefied; the atrocious slime I poured out into the sandy backyard of our holiday house had no relation to the extraordinary creature I had found on the beach. I felt bad but I never suspected that in killing one, I might have contributed to killing them all.

Five years after that, on the same beach, I stood at the top of a dune on an overcast day heavy with coming rain and watched my father running below, pursued by the dog. In his singlet and shorts he looked both skinny and paunchy—suddenly middle-aged—and he was wheezing and puffing even as he laughed like a child, the dog nipping at his heels. I was pierced by twin arrows of love and fear, afraid he might fall, that his heart might fail, afraid to see the old man in him, the first shadow of death. There is no-one to save us, I saw. We are all children.

Ben and I wander along a dun-coloured beach near Port Douglas. On the wide flat sand, the worms one never sees have left their little spiralled sand-turds by the million, evidence of the vast hidden industry of life. We walk into mangroves stinking and gnat-ridden, and find the remains of a bird: white knotted bones, ants in the sandy shrivel of flesh. Ben pauses to look, serious, his mind turning in some deep way, understanding something.

We push deeper into the smelly tidal swamp. I scare Ben just enough with crocodile stories to inject the right expeditionary frisson, and he digs joyfully with a stick among the jabbing mangrove roots. I sit higher up on the ground where some hardy beach succulent keeps my bum dry. My hand finds a rusty hook and a sinker, still tied to the sand by a line like a couch grass root, a thin unbreakable garrotte leading towards the sea.

At sixteen weeks, the ultrasound—I guess I'd prevaricated long enough that the decision had made itself, or Maddy had made it without me. The doctor lifted Maddy's shirt and smeared conductive gel over the tightening drum of her skin. On a screen, snow-storm static turned liquid and something began to take shape, some odd fish that rolled and transformed as the doctor slid her magic device around the shiny brown curves of Maddy's belly. We heard an aquatic heart beat, a rapid pulsing boom like Morse from a far galaxy, life discovered in Andromeda. Then she found the right angle and the child appeared, sucking its minute thumb, its spine as fine and fragile as a sardine's. For a span of unknown heartbeats my breath was stolen, *ohmygodprotectit*. How stupid had I been? Oh my god, protect it. And if god won't, then let me try. Let me try.

I take Ben out to the reef. We are going to have fun. We go flying over the waves on a white ferry with engines strong as a jumbo jet's, standing at the prow, drunk with wind and speed as the boat chops and sprays the sea. When we open our mouths to speak we swallow great gallons of air. The impatient ferry cleaves the horizon like an axe. I feel Ben tugging my sleeve. He points, and there below us are dolphins leaping alongside, improbably keeping pace, improbably joyous. In all wild nature they are our only friends, gregarious in spite of everything.

We reach the reef, and everyone begins the mad scramble for masks and snorkels. But even though he can swim and I promise to hold his hand, Ben is afraid. He says he doesn't want to go in the water. But you wait, you wait, I tell him. You won't believe what it's like down there.

I don't care, he says. I want to go back.

We can't go back.

We can sit inside.

Then the phone in my pocket rings. It's Maddy. I turn away from Ben, holding the phone in a little shelter made by my hand against the wind.

Hi, I say.

Hi.

What is it? Have you found a place yet?

Yes, I have. It's only ten minutes away from the house. I'm moving most of my stuff tomorrow. Where are you?

I'm on the Great Barrier Reef.

You having fun?

Come on, Maddy.

Have you told him yet?

I can't. I just ... can't.

Greg, you have to tell him before you come home on Saturday.

I know. I'm going to, okay? Tonight. I just ... I just don't know how to say it, that's all.

But we agreed on what you'd say.

We should have told him before. We should have told him together.

Silence.

Maddy?

I know. We've fucked it up haven't we?

For a while I'm standing there on the deck like a fool, knuckles gripping the silence. Then her voice again, broken: But it's too late now. He has to know before he gets home.

Look, I better go. We're on the Barrier Reef, and I'm not leaving without seeing it.

Please tell him, Greg.

I will, I promise. Bye, Maddy.

I snap the phone shut.

Dad, says Ben.

Yes, sweetie.

I think I want to go in now.

I crouch down in front of him.

Really?

Uh, huh.

Good lad! Let's go get some snorkels!

I fit the mask to his face, careful not to snag his hair. Then I arrange the snorkel and we sit side by side on the platform, our legs dangling in the dark slapping water, in mystery. I hold his hand, small as a starfish.

You ready?

He nods.

And we slide down into the quiet blue.

Acknowledgements

My gratitude to the following people who read, critiqued and improved these stories: Suzie St George, Francesca Collins, Jon Bauer, Jessica Au, Dan Ducrou, Jeff Hoogenboom—and, of course my editor, Linda 'adverb-killer' Godfrey, who somehow put up with me. Thanks also to Louise Swinn and Zoe Dattner for their support along the rocky road of the 'emerging' writer.

Some of the stories in this collection have been published before, sometimes in slightly different forms, as follows:

Angela's Parrots, **Overland 190** and **Adbusters**, vol. 17, 2009

Comrade Vasilii Goes to War, **Wet Ink**, vol. 11, 2008

Eliot's Awakening, **Sleepers Almanac No. 4**, Sleepers Publishing, 2008

Freak, **Sleepers Almanac**, Sleepers Publishing, 2005

Growing Sickness, **Sleepers Almanac No. 7**, Sleepers Publishing, 2011

Salt, **New Australian Stories**, Scribe Publications, 2009

Shock, **Kill Your Darlings**, vol. 2, 2010

Suburban Mystery, **Meanjin**, vol. 68, 2009

The Thief, **Extempore,** vol. 5, 2011

This Old Man, **Award Winning Australian Writing**, Melbourne Books ,2008

Tornado, **Page Seventeen**, 2011

White Summer, **Sleepers Almanac No. 5**, Sleepers Publishing, 2009

Also published by Spineless Wonders:

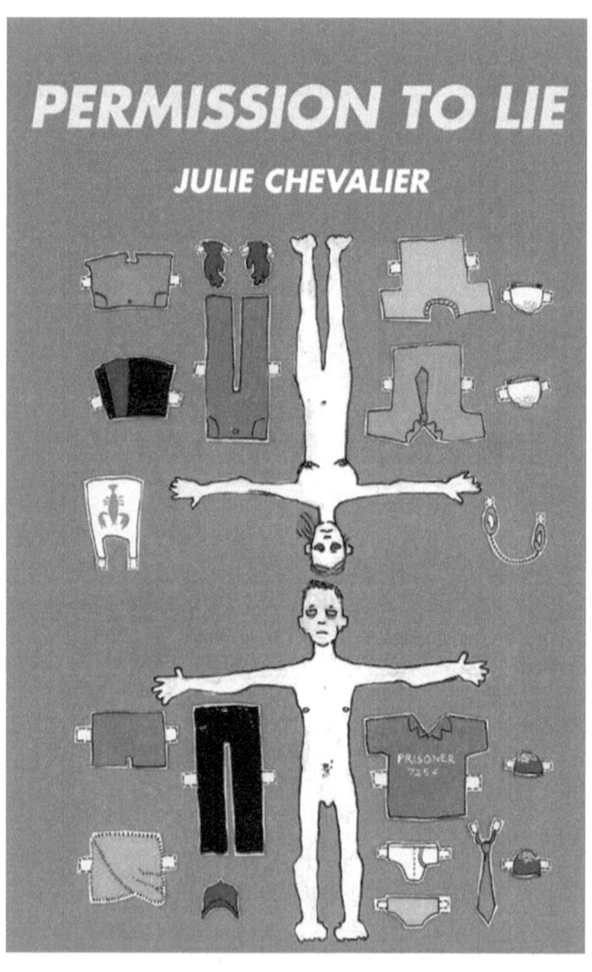

Permission To Lie
by Julie Chevalier

In this wonderfully diverse collection, Chevalier does not flinch from delving into some of the messier aspects of contemporary Australian culture, whether inside prisons, nudist camps or in cut-throat boardrooms.

Cover art and six pages of quirky illustrations by Paden Hunter.

'Holding together the extensive range of this collection is prose of a deceptive simplicity, taut, droll, hinting at greater depths, never giving too much away. A new voice in Australian fiction, wry, gritty, knowing and true.'

Fiona McGregor
author of ***Indelible Ink***

The Rattler
& other stories
A. S. Patrić
"Spare and taut, sometimes tricky, sometimes shocking, yet always
deeply and satisfyingly tender. A great collection."
Paddy O'Reilly

The Rattler

& other stories

by A.S. Patrić

This entertaining collection includes a romp of a novella called *The Rattler*, as well as short stories and micro-fictions all set in and around contemporary Melbourne. Sometimes serious, sometimes seriously playful—always written in breathtakingly beautiful prose—these stories uncover the heartbreaking tragedies, slow-burning emotions and serendipity of ordinary lives.

Cover art and illustrations by Miles Allinson. Collage by Maxine Beneba Clarke.

'An explosive mix of muscular prose and sharp originality. In this collection, A.S. Patrić proves himself to be a writer who must be taken very seriously.'

Vanessa Gebbie
UK author of ***Short Circuit, A Guide to the Art of the Short Story.***

Quality short fiction, packed with surprises.
Prepare to be transported.   Marion Halligan
ESCAPE
An anthology of
short stories

Escape
An anthology of short stories

Here is the thinking person's escapist reading for this summer season. ESCAPE has unexpected tales of contemporary life, comedy, tragedy, mystery, romance, sci-fi, dystopian fantasy, a homage to David Foster Wallace and lots more. All served with a good dose of quirky and a fine turn of phrase.

Features award-winning writers such as Ryan O'Neill, Jen Mills, Andy Kissane, Louise Swinn, Julie Chevalier, A.S. Patrić and Kim Westwood, as well as stories chosen by Sophie Cunningham in the inaugural Carmel Bird Short Fiction Award.

Contains illustrations by talented young artist, Paden Hunter.

www.ingramcontent.com/pod-product-compliance
Lightning Source LLC
Chambersburg PA
CBHW050338110726
47899CB00007B/2547